# GHOSTS OF DEVERAUX MANOR

CARA MARSI

THE PAINTED LADY PRESS

Published by The Painted Lady Press

United States of America

First Electronic Edition: December 2019

Cover by Harris Channing

Formatting by Aileen Fish

Cover copy created by BlurbWriter.com

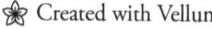 Created with Vellum

Philadelphian Charlotte—Charli—Deveraux had no idea she had relatives in France until she receives notice she's inherited a chateau in Normandy. Her art history degree has led to nothing but a soul-sucking bank job, so she takes leave, and, with her best friend, heads to France to check out the centuries-old manor. But her inheritance comes with more than she expected, including an enticing, maddening neighbor. She'd been betrayed by a man once. She's not about to trust another one.

International art restorer and expat Brit, Travis Gardner, wants nothing to do with any woman named Deveraux. He'd been married to one. When his ex-wife was murdered, suspicion fell on him. Although he had a strong alibi and was cleared by the police, a cloud hangs over him. It doesn't matter how sweet and wholesome Charli is, he's on the hunt for the real killer. He doesn't have time to help Charli find missing necklaces or the keys to a mysterious locked turret.

But a pair of matchmaking ghosts—and their equally ghostly cat —have other ideas. To get into the good graces of the Big Guy, they need to bring Charli and Travis together, and solve not only his ex-wife's murder, but their own. In a village full of suspects, can Charli and Travis find the keys, the jewels, and the truth before they, too, become ghosts of Deveraux manor?

**A Common Elements Romance Project**

# AUTHOR'S NOTE

*Ghosts of Deveraux Manor* is set almost entirely in Normandy, France. I visited that part of France in June, 2016. The rainy, cool weather and the descriptions of the countryside and the small villages are from my remembrances of that trip.

CHAPTER ONE

*C*harlotte Deveraux dragged her heavy suitcase from the trunk of the taxi. Fumes from the exhaust pipe made her cough. The calendar said June, but her breath visible in the cool, rain-soaked air, said November. She muttered a string of curses at the driver who refused to step out of the vehicle and help. Lightning illuminated the French countryside, followed by the loud crack of thunder. Startled, she dropped to the muddy ground. Her suitcase landed on top of her.

*Welcome to Normandy!*

Her friend Shannon Kosta, in the act of hoisting out her own bag, slipped in the mud and tripped over her. Shannon's backside hit the ground with a thump.

The women struggled to their feet. The cab sped off, its tires kicking up watery sludge, and the open trunk jiggling.

Shannon swept wet hair away from her face. "Wow, Charli, talk about rude."

"He acted like he'd seen a ghost." Charli ran a hand down her muddied jacket, only spreading the dirt. "We should be glad we found anyone to take us out here. As soon as we said we were going to Devereaux Manor, no one would drive us."

"What was that about? We paid that cabbie a small fortune and he left us in the dust, or muck in this case."

"My new pants are ruined. I tried to look stylish for this trip." Charli glanced around. "This sure isn't the France I pictured."

"Me, either. My jacket is ruined, too."

Charli fought tears, brought on by jet lag, sleep-deprivation, and frustration. Things had gone from bad to worse since their red-eye from Philadelphia landed in Paris early that morning.

Shannon scanned Charli and laughed. "You've got mud on your face."

"You're not looking so good yourself. Why are we standing here? Let's get the hell out of this rain and into the house. Once we dry off and have some hot tea, we'll both feel better."

"I need something stronger than tea."

"Let's go." Charli hitched her purse over her shoulder and grabbed the handle of her suitcase. She raised her gaze to Deveraux Manor, her inheritance, rising like a ghostly vision through the rain and mist. A long spruce-lined driveway led to the house. Shivering with cold and anxiety, Charli headed up the cobblestone drive, hauling her bag behind her. Shannon, pulling her own bag, followed.

The wheels of their luggage bumped over the uneven pavement. A warning of worse to come? Charli shook her head. No sleep, the long train trip from Paris to Rouen in Normandy, the jarring taxi drive to the house, and the never-ending rain had her imagination going berserk.

"Does it ever stop raining?" Shannon shouted. "Doesn't Mother Nature know it's June?" Another flash of lightning, followed by a crash of thunder close by made Shannon scream.

The imposing house loomed out of the cloud-filled night sky, waiting for them. Three stories high, the house had a hip roof, with three dormers on the third floor and a tower with a smaller tower, or turret, on the right, its round roof rising above the house. Lightning lit the stone tower, illuminating the narrow windows circling the turret room above it. Granite stones blended with the rain, depressing and ominous. The place would fit perfectly on the cover of a Gothic romance. Charli half expected to find a brooding, dangerous hero waiting inside.

"Thank God. An overhang." Charli sighed with relief when they reached the house. The women dragged their belongings up the steep steps, puffing with the effort. At the top, Charli leaned against the wooden door, grateful for the canopy that gave respite from the downpour. They set their suitcases against the black iron railing.

"Where's the key?" Shannon hopped from foot-to-foot. "I have to dry off and pee, not in that order. I hope the plumbing works."

Charli slid her purse off her shoulder and reached into it for the ring holding the keys the lawyer sent her. He handled the estate of Jeanne Deveraux, a distant relative Charli only discovered when she learned she'd inherited the house. She snatched the keys and held them up. "Here they are."

Gripping the large iron key, she struggled to find the keyhole in the dark. A strong gust of wind whipped through, ripping the keys from her hand. "What the...?"

"What happened?" Shannon asked.

Choking back panic, Charli scanned the steps and around the landing. "The keys are gone."

CHAPTER TWO

*C*harli gulped shallow breaths, fighting her rising alarm. A perfect ending to a horrendous day. She should have stayed in Philadelphia. "How could a ring of heavy iron keys rip out of my hand? We'll have to walk back to the village."

"No way." Shannon shook her head. "That place is at least two miles away. We can't drag ourselves and our luggage in this rain."

A male figure emerged out of the mist. A rain hat, pulled low, obscured most of his face. He said something in French.

Both women jumped.

Charli clutched her purse, ready to throw it at the man. "Who are you?" she said in her fractured French, with more bluster than she felt. She'd read somewhere to never let an attacker see your fear.

"Americans? I might have known," the man said in English with a clipped British accent. He placed one foot on the bottom step. "Who are you and what do you want?"

"Is everyone here rude?" Charli blurted.

"Who are you and what are you doing here?" he asked again.

*Calm, Charli, calm.* She straightened her shoulders, and

would have looked him in the eyes if she could have seen his eyes. "I'm Charlotte Deveraux. I own this place. This is my friend Shannon Kosta. A gust of wind blew the keys out of my hand. They're around here somewhere, but I can't see in this darkness." Despite the weather, the lost keys, and the intimidating man, a burst of pride, like the lightning illuminating the sky, shot through her.

Deveraux Manor. Hers. She'd never owned her own house, never had a connection with her family history. She did now.

"Deveraux? You're one of them?" He spit out the words.

Charli took a step back.

"Yes, she is." Shannon pushed in front of Charli. "You got a problem with that?"

"Shannon, it's okay." Charli turned to the guy. "You haven't told us who you are."

Another man, with a rifle slung over his shoulder, came from the back of the house. The women huddled closer to each other.

"What's this, Travis?" the second man asked the first one. He pointed his flashlight at the women. Rain sparkled in the beams of light. He, too, spoke with a British accent, as polished as the other guy, but with a barely audible roughness. His voice and bearing proclaimed him as older.

"These two say they have the keys to Deveraux, but I wonder if they're trying to break in. That story about the keys disappearing is something the paparazzi would say."

Anger replaced Charli's frustration. "We. Were. Not. Breaking. In. We are not paparazzi. I told you I own this place."

"You're related to Jeanne?" the first guy called Travis asked. "Belanger told me an American had inherited the estate. We don't usually walk around armed, but we heard something that sounded like an explosion, plus we've had some recent break-ins in the area. I promised Belanger I'd watch the place."

"Mister, whoever the hell you are, yes, I inherited the house.

I've lost the keys. A biblical rain is pouring. We're tired and hungry and we don't have time for your rudeness."

"We can't search for your keys tonight," he said in a softer tone. "You'll have to stay at my place and we'll hunt for the keys tomorrow."

"Your place? Who *are* you?"

He bowed slightly. "I'm Travis Gardner, and this is Max." He gestured to the older, shorter man standing next to him, then turned back to the women. "You coming?"

"Not so fast." Charli pushed strands of wet hair back from her face. "Where do you live?"

"I'm your next-door neighbor, at Beliveau Manor."

Charli shivered. "Next door? We didn't see any other houses. Although in this rain, we can't see much."

"My home is about a half-mile away."

"Okay, but we can't go off with two strange men." Charli didn't want to walk into the village in this weather. They might not find a hotel there.

"You know Belanger," Travis said. "Call him. He'll vouch for me."

"Okay, I will." With fingers numb from the cold, Charli lifted her phone from her purse and punched in the attorney's number from her contact list. When he answered, she said, "Hello, Monsieur Belanger. This is Charlotte Deveraux. I'm sorry to call so late. I have a situation."

She listened to him describe the house and the best way to get to it. "No, we're at the house now, but I've temporarily lost the keys. I'm sure we'll find them tomorrow. Travis Gardner and Max are here. They say they live next door, and they've invited us to stay at their place for the night."

Charli nodded her head as Belanger vouched for the two men. "*Merci. Bonne nuit.*" She disconnected the call and turned to Travis. "He says you're an okay guy and trustworthy."

Without answering, Travis turned and walked away, Max behind him.

The women looked at each other. "We spend the night here in the rain, or we go with them," Charli said.

"Not really a choice, is it?" Shannon answered.

"We're coming," Charli called.

They grabbed their luggage and sloshed through the rain to catch up with the men. To her surprise, Travis stopped and took her suitcase. Max did the same for Shannon.

Dread pressed against Charli's chest. Normandy, France, in the middle of a thunderstorm following men they just met. But Monsieur Belanger said they were safe with Gardner. She'd never met the attorney, but she trusted him. He'd been helpful from the beginning, when he'd contacted her about the inheritance. She'd also Googled him and found he was one of the best estate lawyers in Normandy.

They trudged along a narrow path, paved with Belgium blocks, for about fifteen minutes when lightning sizzled overhead, revealing a house directly in front of them. Dark and daunting, the house was smaller than Deveraux Manor with no tower to give it a fairy-tale image. Darkness descended again, cloaking the house back into the shadows.

Another bolt of lightning lit a circular drive that fronted stone steps and double wooden doors. Max pushed ahead of the others and climbed the steps, lifting Shannon's suitcase as if it weighed less than a feather. Travis gestured for the women to go next. He brought up the rear. Max opened the doors, then swept an arm out for them to enter.

The women exchanged looks. "Dracula's castle?" Shannon whispered.

"It'll be okay," Charli said. "Monsieur Belanger reassured me we had nothing to fear from Travis and Max."

Once inside the massive foyer, Max shut the doors. The

sound of the heavy doors closing made Charli whirl around. She swallowed the panic clogging her throat.

"I'll show you to your room," Travis said. "Max will bring your bags. You'll find towels in the bathroom to dry off."

Without waiting for them, he strode to the stairs to the left of the foyer. Max grabbed the handles of both bags and stepped aside to allow the women to follow Travis.

Charli had a glimpse of a crystal chandelier hanging from the high ceiling in the entry hall. Carved wooden benches that looked like antiques were set along the wood-paneled walls.

They went up wide carpeted stairs to a long hallway, the floors covered with Oriental rugs that looked expensive and old. Charli's art history degree told her the furniture in the foyer and the Oriental rugs were priceless.

Travis led them to a room at the end of the hall and opened a door. He hit the light switch, flooding the room with brightness, and gestured them inside. His upper face was still obscured by the hat, but the overhead light exposed full lips and a firm jaw.

Kissable lips. The thought came unbidden. Charli's face heated.

Max wheeled in their luggage and left.

Travis pointed to an antique key set into a brass lock. "That's the only key, and it locks from the inside." He turned on his heel and walked out.

Her hazel eyes wide, Shannon stared at the closed door, then back to Charli. "We're in a real-life vampire movie. Travis is Dracula and Max is his zombie servant."

"You read too many vampire romances and watch too many horror movies. It's an old house, not a vampire's castle." Despite her reassuring words, a shiver ran up Charli's spine. "We're still locking the door."

# CHAPTER THREE

*C*harli threw her purse on the queen size four-poster and scanned the room. "This place is something."

"Yeah, Dracula's Castle."

"Stop it, Shannon. It may not belong to Dracula but it sure looks like someone with taste owns it. I would have expected heavy dark furniture, not this beautiful Danish stuff, and to have red velvet drapes. That's what you'd find in Dracula's Castle."

Lightning sparked outside, but barely permeated the brocade drapes in shades of beige and green. The bedspread and canopy over the bed matched the drapes. Area rugs in shades of red, green, and beige were spread over dark wood floors. The drapes muffled the claps of thunder and the sound of the rain pelting the windows.

"I see the bathroom through that door." Shannon made a beeline for the other room. "I'll throw you a towel."

Charli caught the towel Shannon threw and attempted to wipe some of the mud off her and to dry her face and hair. She turned to the one bed. "Looks like we share. I'm ready to crash on my feet."

Despite the raging storm, exhaustion and jet lag helped

Charli sleep well. Awake and refreshed, she opened her eyes and sat up. Sun peeked through the slim openings in the heavy curtains. Sunshine at last.

She slipped from the bed, walked to the windows, and pushed open the brocade drapes to expose sheer white ones beneath. When she slid them aside, she gasped at the scene spread out below. Sunlight shone on lush green rolling hills leading to a low stone wall. They must have come in another way last night because even in the rain she would have noticed the wall. The small village of Deveraux sparkled in the distance like a fairy land. Once she settled into Deveraux Manor, she'd walk into the quaint-looking village. Their train from Paris had let them off in Rouen, the nearest city. After much haggling and begging, they'd secured a driver willing to take them to Deveraux. Barely.

The taxi drivers at the station enthusiastically vied for the women's business, until Charli mentioned they needed transport to Deveraux Manor. The drivers made signs of the cross, shook their heads, and walked away.

Her stomach rumbled, reminding her she hadn't eaten since yesterday afternoon on the train. The bedside clock said eight. She wanted coffee and food, but first, a much-needed shower. She turned back to the bed and shook Shannon awake.

"What time is it?" Shannon sat up and pushed hair out of her eyes.

"Eight. I'm starving and dying for coffee. Let's hope Gardner's hospitality extends to breakfast. I'm jumping in the shower, then you can get in."

At nine, the women were dressed and their suitcases ready. Charli had her hand on the doorknob when someone knocked. She cautiously opened the door to find an elderly woman outside.

The woman gestured for them to come out. "*Venez manger.*"

Charli glanced at Shannon. "She said, 'Come eat.'"

"Sounds good to me. We can leave our suitcases, but we'd

better grab our purses. They have our passports, money, and phones."

"Good idea."

Purses in hand, they followed the woman along the hall and down the stairs. At the bottom, they made two left turns.

"I couldn't find my way out of here," Shannon whispered to Charli.

Charli put a finger to her mouth. "Shush."

The woman took them to a spacious kitchen with a black and white tile floor and stainless appliances. A wooden farm table had been set with napkins, plates, flatware, and mugs. A fireplace, large enough for a person to stand in, took up one wall. A roaring fire in the hearth gave the kitchen a cozy feel and warmed the room.

The elderly woman pointed toward the table, and Charli and Shannon sat.

Charli's gaze swept the room. "I didn't expect a modern kitchen here. This place is filled with surprises."

"Dracula is fattening us up for the kill. Our blood will be richer after we eat."

"Stop that."

A tray holding jars of jam and a plate piled high with flaky croissants was on the table. The woman placed a large carafe in front of them before she shuffled out.

"French breakfast," Charli said. "It all looks delicious." She pulled the carafe closer and poured two mugs of coffee.

Shannon grabbed a croissant and dropped it into her plate. Charli did the same.

They ate in silence. Charli was hungrier than she thought. Finally, filled with the simple, but tasty meal, she pushed away her empty plate. "That was amazing." Sipping coffee, she settled back in her chair.

Heavy footsteps sounded close, drawing their attention toward the door.

Charli almost dropped her mug when the source of the footsteps entered. Her pulse double-timed. The hottest man she'd ever seen stood there scowling at them, his dark green eyes, framed by thick black lashes, narrowed.

Black hair, a trifle too long, curled around his ears. The light stubble on his firm jaw gave him a hipster vibe. He appeared to be in his mid-thirties, not much older than her twenty-nine. Dark washed jeans showcased legs that went on forever. His blue dress shirt, untucked, stretched over impossibly broad shoulders. Opened at the neck, the shirt revealed a smattering of dark hairs.

Unable to look away from such awesomeness, Charli slowly set down her mug.

"Miss Deveraux. Miss Kosta. I trust you slept well." His British accent and deep, rich voice gave him away. This was Travis Gardner. Nice!

"We slept very well, thank you," Charli said. "Please call me Charli. Everyone does."

Shannon stared up at him, her face lighting with appreciation. "Breakfast was good, too. Call me Shannon."

The servant woman lumbered back into the kitchen and spoke in rapid French to Travis. He shook his head and pointed to the carafe. The woman left. He pulled down a mug from a cabinet and poured himself coffee.

Tense silence filled the room. Unable to sit still, Charli stood. "I guess we'd better get our things. Thanks for helping last night. We need to find our keys."

"Max will escort you back and help you." Holding his mug, Travis walked to the doorway, then looked back. "Be careful of the ghosts of Deveraux Manor."

The women watched his retreating figure.

"Ghosts?" Shannon squeaked out. "He's hot, but he's scaring me with that talk of ghosts."

"Forget it. He's being a jerk and trying to frighten us. I doubt we'll see much of him in the month we're here. Once the manor is ready to sell, it's back to Philadelphia."

"Hot and sunny Philadelphia. Never thought I'd miss the heat and humidity so much."

They retraced their steps to the entry hall and found Max waiting for them. Middle-aged, barrel chested, with broad shoulders and a trim waist, his gray hair cut military style, he reminded Charli of a friend of her dad's who'd spent twenty years in the Army.

Max's thin lips tilted in a slight smile. "I put your suitcases in the car. We'll take the road back to Deveraux Manor."

They followed him out the front door to a late-model Mercedes idling in the driveway.

<><><>

Travis sat in his study and finished his coffee. He'd needed this break from his hectic work pace, but the inactivity of the past months had begun to grate on him. No large art restoration projects had come his way lately, but he wasn't ready yet for an overseas assignment that would keep him away for months. To stay busy, maybe he'd start taking small jobs close to his home here.

Although the police had cleared him of Louise's murder, he didn't want to leave the country until they caught the killer. If the police weren't doing much to find the murderer, he would do it. He owed it to Jeanne, a good person, unlike her grand-niece Louise, his ex-wife.

He set his mug on the desk and leaned back in his chair, his hands behind his head. He'd acted like a jerk to the American women last night and just now. At the rumblings coming from Deveraux Manor, he'd feared an explosion. When he saw two women standing on the steps, he'd been sure they were reporters who'd gotten lost looking for his place. God knows, he'd had enough reporters hounding him in the six months since his ex-wife's murder.

Seeing Charlotte, or Charli, standing on the steps of Deveraux had made him lash out at her in shock. He was sure he was seeing Louise's ghost.

Charli was a stunner, with her dark brown hair and blue-gray eyes. It wasn't her fault she bore a striking resemblance to Louise.

He didn't know what had prompted him to mention the ghosts to Charli and Shannon. Although the suspicious inhabitants in the village swore spirits haunted Deveraux Manor, and Louise had told him stories of weird noises in the old house when she lived there with her great-aunt Jeanne, he didn't believe any of it. He'd reacted on a visceral level to Charli, scaring her about the spirits.

Charli was a Deveraux.

Deveraux women couldn't be trusted.

# CHAPTER FOUR

*T*hey arrived at Deveraux Manor, and Shannon and Charli parked their suitcases outside by the front door.

Charli rubbed her hands together. "Where should we start our search?"

Max shrugged. "They couldn't have gone far."

"I'll start with these bushes near the steps," Charli said. "They're thick so it would be easy for something to disappear in there."

"I'll search the bushes on the other side," Shannon answered.

Charli turned to Max. "How about you cover the drive closest to the house?"

A soft breeze brushed Charli's forehead and she heard chuckling. Frowning, she glanced toward Shannon, but the other woman was busy parting the shrubbery to the right of the steps. Max, head down, ambled in a circle examining the walkway. The chuckling came from the roof. Charli raised her gaze. Nothing was there. Her jet lag must be worse than she thought.

Max helped them look through the large bushes that obscured the first-floor windows. All three had scratches on their hands from the sharp branches, but they found nothing. Frustration knotted Charli's chest. She sat on the bottom step, her shoulders sagging.

Shannon plopped down next to her. "What happened to those keys?"

Max leaned against the iron railing. "I doubt the keys could have blown far, but we'll expand our search to the sides and back."

Charli met Max's gaze. "While we're taking a break, I have some questions, if you don't mind."

He stayed silent.

Strange guy. As strange as his hot, but maddening, boss. "Max, you work for Travis?"

"I grew up with his father in London." Max's features softened. "I've known Travis his whole life. When he moved to Normandy, he offered me the position of his estate manager. He is often gone on business and needs someone to look out for things here."

Charli tilted her head and studied him. She wanted to ask what kind of business Travis did, but felt that was too intrusive. She wouldn't be in France long enough to find out or care. "One more question. We had a hard time finding a taxi to drive us from Rouen. As soon as we said we needed to go to Deveraux Manor, the drivers refused to take us. Travis told us to be careful of the ghosts. What's that about?"

Max blinked and his features tightened. "The taxi drivers are silly peasants. Travis was repeating talk from the villagers. He meant nothing. I'm sure he didn't mean to scare you."

The sound of metal hitting stone made all three jerk their attention toward the pathway that led between Deveraux Manor and Beliveau, Travis's house. Glinting in the sun lay the ring of keys.

Chills ran up Charli's spine. She stood slowly. "What the...? Those weren't there a minute ago."

Shannon looked upward. "Maybe they were in a tree and a gust of wind blew them down."

"There was no gust of wind." Charli strode to the keys and snatched them before they could disappear again. Holding them up triumphantly, she grinned at the others.

"I'll stay until I'm sure you can get in." Max walked to the car and stood by it.

Charli climbed the steps and put the iron key into the keyhole and turned it. The door swung open on squeaky hinges.

"Thanks, Max." Charli waved to him. Max got into the car and drove away.

Nervousness tightened Charli's chest. "Let's see what Great-Aunt Jeanne left me."

Grabbing her suitcase handle, Charli pushed the heavy wooden door open wider and stepped over the marble threshold. "Wow! Nice!"

"This place could fit into the Main Line," Shannon said, naming Philadelphia's wealthiest neighborhood. She crowded in behind Charli.

Although the exterior reminded Charli of a gothic castle from some gloomy movie, the interior was open concept with light wood floors and scattered area rugs in modern geometric prints in shades of white, gray, and turquoise. The large foyer, furnished with a hat stand, a chair upholstered in a turquoise and gray geometric print, and a small tile-topped table with red roses in a crystal vase, was bigger than Charli's bathroom in her apartment in Philadelphia.

She walked over to the flowers and read the card. "From Monsieur Belanger. How nice. I wish my dad could have seen this house. He would have been so proud." Her throat thickened.

"This place is beautiful. The photos the attorney sent, and the pictures we saw on the Internet don't do it justice." Shannon ran her fingers over the gray wall. "I can't wait to check out the six bedrooms, wine cellar, sun room, and especially that turret room."

"You sound like a real estate agent," Charli said, smiling at her.

Shannon put a hand on her hip. "Aren't you happy I talked you into coming? You were going to let the lawyer sell the place sight unseen by you."

"Despite all we went through yesterday, I'm glad we're here. I've never traveled out of the United States before, and I was a little afraid."

"You are too damn cautious, girlfriend."

Charli touched Shannon's arm. "Thanks for coming with me."

"Wouldn't miss it. What kind of friend would I be if I didn't give my best friend moral support? Plus, I have an ulterior motive. Since I can work from anywhere and Skype with my employees, it's no biggie to get away. That client my company is wooing is in London. If I need to go see him to close the deal, I'm almost there."

"Why are we standing here?" Charli asked. "Let's see the rest of the place. I only have a one-month leave from work so there's not much time to get the estate settled to sell."

The foyer spilled into a spacious living room on the right, furnished in groupings of sofas and sectionals upholstered in a nubby gray fabric. The walls were painted pale pewter with white baseboards and wainscoting. A fireplace with a white marble mantel stood as the focal point.

"This is so HGTV," Charli said.

Leaving their suitcases in the foyer, the women strolled into the room. Charli went to the Palladian windows and opened the airy white drapes, letting in the weak sun. Thank God the place didn't appear like a version of Dracula's castle. For sure, Shannon would have gone running out.

"Great-Aunt Jeanne had a good sense for decorating." A

painting on the wall across the room caught Charli's eye and made her gasp. "That can't be a Frank Stella."

"Seriously? A Stella here?"

Charli hurried over to the artwork and examined it. She'd studied enough art to recognize the real thing, and this was a genuine Stella.

"It's real," she said, turning to Shannon.

"Wow!" Shannon moved to the painting and stared up at it. "I've only seen one of his paintings at the Philadelphia Art Museum."

"It must be worth a small fortune. I'll call Chloe later. She'll be excited to know I own a Stella."

"With the sale of the painting and this house, you might finally be able to quit your job and go in with Chloe."

"So long as the estate taxes don't take all the money." A manager at a local bank, work she hated, Charli found pleasure from her part-time position at her friend Chloe Decker DiMarco's art gallery in Philadelphia's Society Hill. She hoped with the sale of the house and grounds she could escape her soul-crushing job and buy into Chloe's gallery.

Charli spun slowly around, studying their surroundings. "Along with that painting and what it must have cost to decorate and restore this place, you'd think Jeanne was sitting on a lot of old family money. Monsieur Belanger said she had just enough in her savings to pay her funeral expenses. Sad. Maybe her grandniece spent all the money."

"Spent it on the couture clothes and designer shoes and bags in the niece's closet, all unused, according to Belanger. I'd say she liked to spend money. Let's find the bedrooms and park our bags." Shannon turned toward the entry and the stairs off to the side.

Charli started to follow when something large and white ran past. Surprise made her scream, but whatever it was disappeared.

"What's wrong?" Shannon asked.

"Did you see that thing run by?"

"What thing? Was it a rat? Please don't let it be a rat."

"It resembled a cat."

"Cat? Here? Alone? Your jet lag is making you hallucinate."

"Probably."

The bedrooms were as airy and elegant as the living room. A set of narrow stairs led to the third floor. Two small rooms were on that floor, one filled with boxes, evidently used for storage, and the other with a desk and several chairs. The tower entrance was on that floor, but the door was locked. Too tired to bother with it, Charli and Shannon decided to explore the tower with its turret room the next day, figuring the key had to be on the ring the attorney had given Charli.

The second floor had four suites with ensuite bathrooms, and two large bedrooms with a shared bathroom between them. The women settled into two of the suites. Each had a spacious bedroom, a comfortable sitting room, and a marble bathroom larger than Charli's study at home.

While Shannon, jet-lagged, took a nap, Charli sat at the granite peninsula in the open, modern white and gray kitchen sipping a cup of hot mint tea. Like the kitchen at Travis Gardner's Beliveau, the room boasted a fireplace with a natural wood mantel.

The refrigerator was stocked with enough food for a few days, another welcome from Belanger. She'd have to add a little something to his commission to thank him for his help.

"Wish I could take this whole place back to Philly with me," Charli announced to the empty and silent room. "Think of the great parties I'd throw." Her entire apartment could fit into this kitchen.

A sudden chill descended over her. She glanced around to check if a window or vent was opened. Everything appeared closed tight. She shivered and wrapped her hands around the hot mug. She wondered if it ever got warm here. At least it had stopped raining.

She grabbed one of the buttered croissants she'd found in the refrigerator and bit into it. According to the box with the pastries, they came from a bakery in the village. Later, she'd walk into town to check it out and buy more croissants, and some macarons, her favorite French pastry. If only Tim Sheehan could see her now. The rat bastard would regret he'd dumped her.

Thinking of Tim opened the wound in her heart. Although there hadn't been much passion between them, she'd thought she loved him, and that he'd felt the same. Together since freshman year in high school, they'd had a comfortable relationship and planned to marry. He did get married, but to someone else. He'd neglected to tell his fiancée, Charli, ahead of his nuptials.

She rubbed her forehead as if she could scrub away the hurt and betrayal. That had happened two years ago almost to the day. The Tim she'd known all those years had been a stable, quiet guy. There were times she suspected he wanted more from their relationship, but he never said. She didn't believe he'd ever cheated on her. Until he did, and married the woman he'd cheated with. Had he found passion with that woman, something he'd never had with Charli?

Tim faded from her mind as Travis Gardner's image came into focus. He'd been gruff and rude at times, but helped them last night. Pleasant to them this morning, he almost redeemed himself in her eyes until he made the snarky remark about ghosts.

# CHAPTER FIVE

The sun began its descent in the cloudless sky as Charli slipped on her jacket and slung her purse over her shoulder, locking the door behind her. She itched to check out the village, to do more than sit around. Shannon, a V-P at a graphic arts company, refreshed from her nap, worked on her laptop and couldn't join her. Charli stood on the top step and breathed in the June air, perfumed with flowers.

In the rain and the dark last night, she'd not had a chance to peruse the property. Undulating green hills framed the stone chateau. Tall trees, swaying gently in the breeze, lined the long driveway. Before she left Deveraux Manor to return to Philly, she'd sketch pictures of the house and the ruined castle tower that was part of the property. Shannon was right—the photos Belanger sent didn't do the manor or surrounding area justice.

Glad she'd worn her high-top sneakers, she headed down the cobblestone drive. The trees provided a leafy canopy. Halfway down, she turned to the house, standing majestically, mistress of all it surveyed. Charli shivered, remembering the something white that had run past her and the sudden chill earlier in the kitchen. Travis's words about ghosts came back to her. She didn't believe in ghosts or in silly rumors about them.

Like strokes of pale paint, muted sunbeams brushed the manor, highlighting the varying shades of brown in the stone. Charli half expected Rapunzel to stream her long blonde hair from one of the turret windows. Two chimneys thrust up from the roof. The artist in her found joy in the asymmetrical beauty of the house, with five rectangular windows on the second floor, and seven long windows on the first floor.

It truly was a stately edifice, and it belonged to her, at least for a while. She couldn't afford the upkeep, and her home was in Philadelphia.

She continued her stroll, thankful for the sun in rainy Normandy. The rustling of the trees surrounded her like a symphony. She wrapped her jacket tighter around her. An odd sensation of being watched made her stop and scan the area. She saw no one. Shaking her head at her fanciful thoughts, she headed into the tiny hamlet, about two miles away, nestled in the valley.

Deveraux Village consisted of one main street with several smaller streets shooting off from the center. Narrow wooden buildings huddled together, much as they had since the Middle Ages.

She stopped, again feeling something or someone watched. She gazed upward. The ruined tower of Deveraux Castle kept guard from the top of a hill. The trek to the ruins appeared challenging, but she would visit before she left for home.

Her shopping took almost two hours as she meandered through the town, taking her time, enjoying the quaint village. When she'd said her name to the shop owners, she'd encountered wariness, but they'd been friendly. Happily loaded with bags carrying fresh-baked baguettes, macarons, croissants, delicious cheeses, fresh fish, and two filet mignons, Charli decided to ask the cheese monger, her last stop for the day, for a recommendation for someone to come out to the manor to give it a good cleaning. The house wasn't messy, but Monsieur Belanger had had it cleaned once in the six months since Jeanne's death, and Charli felt it needed another going-over.

At Charli's question, in French, the middle-aged woman widened her eyes in fright and stepped back.

"What's wrong?" Maybe she'd inadvertently used the wrong words. Charli pulled her phone from her purse and activated her translator app to ask again. She provoked the same response. The woman held up her hands. Charli expected her to make a cross with her fingers like they did against witches and vampires in horror movies.

"Miss Deveraux." At the male voice, familiar, sexy, deep, and British, behind her, she whirled around. Her eyes collided with a broad masculine chest covered in a navy sweater. She lifted her gaze to meet the dark green eyes of Travis Gardner.

"Miss Deveraux. Do you need help?"

Charli swallowed, finding her voice. "My French is very bad and I don't think she understands what I asked. Please call me Charli."

"What did you ask, Charli?"

The way he said her name, his accent a caress, sent a thrill through her. "I need to hire workers to clean Deveraux Manor. It's not dirty, but I'd like it freshened up."

His lips curved in the beginnings of a smile he quickly suppressed. "I'll see what I can do."

He greeted the woman behind the counter and began speaking French. Charli smiled at the woman, hopeful she'd get the help she needed.

"Non, non," the woman said, crossing her arms over her chest.

Travis said something else. Charli heard the woman say, "*hanté*."

Charli's French was bad, but she was sure the word meant "haunted." She gulped, fighting the anxiety racing through her.

The woman continued to shake her head. Shrugging, Travis met Charli's gaze. "I'll send the cleaning people I use over to your chateau tomorrow."

"Thank you."

His attention swiveled to the bags she carried. "Need help with those? I'm heading back to Beliveau."

"Okay. That's good of you. Thank you for helping with the cleaning crew. Did you have something to do here in town before we go back?"

"Nothing. I've been walking for a while, enjoying the rare sun. I suddenly found myself in the village. I hadn't intended to come this way, but it's good I did, for your sake."

He held out his hands for the packages and she gave him all but the smallest. Without a word, he turned and left the shop. She hurried to catch up. His long legs could cover ground much faster than her shorter ones.

"What time should I expect this crew tomorrow?" she asked. "How much do they charge?"

"They should arrive early, around eight. Don't worry about payment. I've been using them for a long time. I'll pay, as a welcome gift to you."

Charli stopped. "That's really nice of you, but I can pay."

Travis stopped too, and shifted the bags he held. "It's nothing. We help each other around here."

"Very neighborly of you," she said. "I'm only going to be here one month, and if I need them a second time, I *will* pay."

He frowned. "As you wish. You're not staying?"

"I wanted to visit the place I inherited, but I plan to put it up for sale. I can't afford to keep it. The taxes alone would cripple me. Until one month ago, I had no idea I had relatives here. My parents never spoke of them. Apparently, Jeanne Deveraux knew about us. Monsieur Belanger said she had a grand-niece, Louise, who died around the same time as she did. Under French law, the bulk of the estate would have gone to the niece or her heirs. He tells me the niece had no heirs."

"That's true."

Charli shrugged. "Jeanne's will directed if there were no heirs in France, the estate would go to whatever members of the Deveraux family were in the United States. Here I am, the last living Deveraux. If none of us were found, the estate was to go to charity. Although I didn't know Jeanne or the grand-niece, I feel sorry they died."

A shadow crossed Travis's face. Without another word, he hefted her bags and continued walking.

<><><>

Two ghosts materialized in a tree high above Charli and Travis. "That went well, don't you think?" Andre asked his wife.

Dominique brushed her fingernails on her shoulder, then examined them. "Couldn't have gone better. Good plan I had to entice Travis to come into town."

Andre laughed. "Yes, you deserve the credit for getting him to town, but I made those keys blow away last night."

"And I caused the noise that brought Travis to Deveraux in the storm."

"This is not a competition, ma cherie. We have a mission, and we will complete it. This time."

Dominque shuddered. "I cannot go back to that place."

"We will not have to, love. Have faith."

# CHAPTER SIX

Shannon and Charli prepared a dinner of cheese omelets, soup, and baguettes. A rich burgundy they'd discovered in a small cellar accompanied their meal. The wine was a name Charli recognized on sale at the village wine shop. Other bottles in the cellar had labels that told her they were more valuable. She wouldn't open them.

"This is good stuff." Shannon reached for the bottle and topped off her glass. "I hope you're not considering leaving all that wine for the new owners."

Charli laughed. "Do you really think it would still be here after all those realtors and prospective buyers came through? I plan to have the liquor appraised and sell it before we leave, along with those couture clothes that belonged to the grand-niece, the ones Monsieur Belanger put into storage. Hopefully, from those items, I'll make enough to pay the estate taxes."

"When is Belanger giving you the list of the items Jeanne had appraised?"

"He said soon. He's having his accountant go over it to estimate how much in taxes I'll have to pay. He's also contacting Sotheby's to arrange an auction of the more valuable things I don't want. Once I have the itemization, I'll get a better idea of what's in this house, but in the meantime, we can continue our search and catalogue what we find." Charli pushed up from her chair. "Let's go to that tower and the turret room. We may discover things not included in the appraisal."

They climbed the stairs and stood before the wooden door to the round tower with the turret. The overhead lamp highlighted the elaborate carving of a stag that decorated the door. "This door is exquisite. Wonder why they hid it up here." Charli rubbed a hand along the two rusted iron hinges that ran halfway across the door. "These look like they'd fall apart with a little tug. We'd better be careful." She pulled the key ring out of her pocket and tried one of the keys, brass like the lock. It wouldn't turn. She tried the handle. It didn't budge. She then tried all the keys, but the door held fast. "I can't believe none of these worked." She brushed a frustrated hand over her hair.

Confusion flitted across Shannon's face. "Why would this room be locked anyway? None of the bedrooms were."

"I'm sure there's a reasonable explanation." Despite her words, doubt shuddered through Charli. "It's getting late and we're still jet-lagged. We'll search tomorrow in daylight. The key could be in a drawer somewhere."

Shannon yawned. "I'm gonna go to my room and relax."

"Me, too."

The women trudged down to their rooms. A light breeze drifted over Charli. She hugged herself and whirled around, but the hall was empty.

Chilled, she went into the suite she'd selected. Darkness shrouded the room. Odd. She'd left on a light before they went up to the third floor. She walked to the night table and clicked on the small lamp, half expecting the bulb had burned out. But the light shone brightly. Charli rubbed her palms along her upper arms. She'd been in a hurry to go to the turret. Maybe she hadn't left the lamp on after all.

Ignoring the fluttering in her stomach that signaled something was amiss, she sat on the bed and pulled off her sneakers, then her jeans and sweater. She put the sweater in a dresser drawer and hung the jeans in the walk-in closet that was bigger than her entire bedroom at home. She set her sneakers on top of the loose floorboards she'd discovered in the closet, and wondered again why no one had fixed those loose boards.

Standing in the closet doorway, she looked out to the luxurious bedroom. Painted pale gray with white trim, same as the downstairs, this room was furnished in light wood pieces with a vanity table and mirror in a niche cut into the room. The *ensuite* bathroom held a white soaking tub and a separate shower, big enough for two. She wouldn't be taking a shower with anyone, that was for sure.

Images of Travis Gardner scrolled through her mind like paintings on a wall. She wondered if his body was as firm and muscled as it seemed. She shook her head, trying to dislodge her wayward thoughts. She didn't need a man in her life now. It would be a long time before she learned to trust again.

Dressed in pajamas, her Kindle® in hand, she settled into a comfortable chair in the adjoining sitting room to read a new romance from her favorite author before falling into bed. The sitting room held a loveseat and chair upholstered in the same nubby gray fabric as the sofas in the living room. A low table in pale wood was set in front of the sofa, and to the side was a table and two chairs, the perfect setting for a light meal.

She read for a while, then yawning, she set down the book and went to bed. Deep in sleep later, the thump of something falling onto the bed woke Charli. She jumped up, afraid of what she might see. Her breathing shallow, she held the sheets to her chest. A white cat sat close and washed itself. "Who are you…?"

The feline blinked yellow eyes and disappeared. Charli screamed.

"What's wrong?" Shannon banged on Charli's bedroom door, then flung it open. She stood on the threshold. "Are you okay?"

Charli pushed hair back from her face with a hand that shook. "I had a dream that seemed so real. I saw a cat. I'm okay. Go back to sleep."

"You're sure?"

"Yes. Go."

Alone again, Charli focused on the spot where the cat had been. That animal was real. And it vanished like a puff of smoke. Those stories about the manor being haunted might not be peasant tales.

She huddled back in the bed, the covers pulled up to her neck. She. Did. Not. Believe. In. Ghosts.

<><><>

"Mon Ange, you are a naughty girl." Dominique stroked Angel when the cat appeared beside her while the ghosts relaxed in the sunroom.

"You should keep the cat away from Charli," Andre said. "We don't want Charli leaving early out of fright. We need to complete our mission. Or else."

"Mon Ange is too sweet to scare anyone. Don't worry. We will do our job." Dominique looked to the ceiling. "We must keep our deal with the Big Guy."

<><><>

The doorbell rang at eight the next morning. Charli set down her mug of coffee and headed out of the kitchen to answer. Voices in French wafted from the other side of the closed front door. She opened it to five women, four young, twenty-some-thing, and the fifth, middle-aged.

"You're the housekeeping crew?" Charli said in her bad French.

"Oui," the middle-aged woman said. "Mr. Gardner, he send us."

Relieved the woman spoke English, Charli moved aside to let them in. The older woman marched past her but the younger ones sidled in, clutching their cleaning materials, their eyes wide and frightened.

*Oh, for God's sake. There are no spirits here.* Charli wanted to say the words out loud, but she kept a smile on her face and ushered them into the living room. The white cat on her bed popped into her mind. That was a dream. Yet, the cat had seemed so real.

"I'm Charli," she said.

The older one pointed to her chest. "Lucie."

Charli nodded at Lucie. "Okay. Let me show you what I need cleaned."

Lucie said something to the others, then followed Charli out of the room. The younger women stayed behind, clustered together.

Charli took Lucie through the rooms she wanted cleaned—the suites she and Shannon used, the kitchen, the living room, study, and sunroom.

Once the crew began working, Charli dragged out her laptop, thankful the manor had Wi-Fi, and sat at the kitchen peninsula. Shannon was using the room with the desk and chairs on the third floor as her office. The cleaning crew's chatter kept Charli company, a slash of normalcy that calmed her.

She opened her search engine and typed in "Travis Gardner." Obviously wealthy and living in a castle-type house in Normandy, he intrigued her.

She expected to scroll through several Travis Gardners before she found her neighbor. To her surprise, his name popped up first.

She clicked on the link. The first photo was one of him surrounded by French police. A lump formed in her throat. The caption had her gasping.

*International art restorer Travis Gardner being taken to the police station in Rouen, France, for questioning in the murder of his former wife Louise Deveraux Gardner.*

Murder? Louise Deveraux Gardner. Jeanne's grand-niece? It had to be.

Her nearest neighbor, Travis, a murderer? She read on to learn the authorities didn't have enough evidence to hold him, especially as he'd been out of the country when Louise was murdered.

Travis Gardner had been married to Charli's relative.

Pulse racing, Charli kept reading. Photos of a younger, happier-looking Travis appeared. In some of the pictures, he was with a familiar-looking stunning raven-haired woman.

She read the caption under a picture of him and the young woman. Her breath hitched and she slid back in her chair.

*Scion of the esteemed Gardners of the United Kingdom, Travis Gardner and his new wife, Louise Deveraux of Deveraux, France.*

"Oh. My. God." Charli pressed a palm to her churning stomach. Charli knew why the woman looked familiar. They resembled each other. Louise's features were more chiseled, with higher cheekbones. Her hair was a few shades darker than Charli's. Taller than Charli, she was slender enough to be a model.

Charli moved closer to the screen and scrolled through the images. Most were of the paintings Travis had restored for collections and private citizens all over the world. An artist, she appreciated his work.

She wondered when he and Louise had gotten divorced. They couldn't have been married long.

Laptop in hand, Charli hurried to the small office where Shannon worked. She smiled at the cleaners she passed in the hall. The young women averted their eyes. Sheesh! You might think she had two heads, or was a ghost.

She knocked on the office door, then entered. Shannon looked up from her computer, a quizzical expression on her face. "Everything okay?"

"Sorry to interrupt, but I have to show you something."

"Holy crap!" Finished reading, Shannon sat back. "Hot neighbor might be a killer? And the victim is your relative, who he was married to? Double holy crap!"

"He's not been charged with anything. No one's saying he murdered her. He wasn't even in France when she was killed."

Shannon lifted an eyebrow. "Wonder why the police won't reveal all the details of how she died."

"The investigators probably hope the killer will trip up so they hide some of the specifics. It gives me the creeps knowing her body was found in the garden at Deveraux Manor. Why didn't Belanger tell me this? Louise was murdered six months ago, around the time Jeanne died. Monsieur Belanger said Jeanne died first. He didn't tell me about the murder."

Shannon rubbed her arms. "I've got goosebumps. Maybe Belanger didn't want to scare you. We're living in a murder scene, or we're in an episode of *Criminal Minds*. The two deaths could be connected."

Charli snapped the lid of her laptop closed. "I don't see anything about Jeanne's death. It's evidently not suspicious."

"If Jeanne died first, it means Louise inherited, then she died. And here we are," Shannon said.

"I know. Fate can be tricky."

# CHAPTER SEVEN

"*I*'ll leave you to your work." Clutching her laptop, Charli started for the door.

"This murdered woman, Louise, is your relative." Shannon said. "Don't you want to know more about her, or who killed her?"

"The investigation could take years." But curiosity ate at Charli. Louise Deveraux was family, even if she'd never met her.

"Open that computer again," Shannon said. "You know you want to."

The women leaned over the screen as Louise Deveraux's face appeared. She'd come up immediately when they entered her name.

"You resemble her," Shannon said. "But she looks a little cold, kind of self-important. You're not like that."

"Thanks. I see the family resemblance. She's very stylish."

Shannon laughed. "Well, yeah, she is, uh, was French after all."

"Here's a picture of Jeanne. Belanger sent me one of her, but not this one." Charli pointed to an elderly woman standing in front of Deveraux Manor. The woman's haughty expression, stylish gray hair, and chic suit shouted money and breeding.

"Look at that necklace Jeanne is wearing. Pearl chain with a pear-shaped diamond pendant. The diamond looks about three carats, the size of the one in my engagement ring." Shannon rolled her eyes. "My mercifully short-lived engagement." She peered closer at the photo. "Unlike my diamond, that necklace must be worth a fortune." Eyes wide, she met Charli's gaze. "That piece of jewelry should be on the list of appraised assets Monsieur Belanger has. We haven't found the necklace, but maybe it's in the turret room, and that's why the door is locked. The necklace belongs to you now. You're the last living Deveraux."

Charli straightened. "We'd better do a more thorough check of this place before it goes on the market."

"Good thinking. You never know what's hidden around here."

"That turret is the only room we haven't seen. We need to get into it. But how? Monsieur Belanger told me he gave me all the keys to the house. And if there's a safe deposit box, Belanger would have told me about it." Charli pulled the laptop closer. "Let's search for more about Travis."

"Wow! The Gardner family is one of the richest in Britain!" Shannon said when they'd finished reading about Travis and his family.

Charli sank into her chair. "Wonder why he didn't go into the family business."

According to what they'd read, Travis's grandfather had founded a land development company that had made him a billionaire. Travis's father and brother ran the operation now.

Shannon shrugged. "He probably finds art more interesting than building houses."

"Could be. Wonder, too, why he didn't go back to the UK when he and Louise got divorced."

"He must like living here."

<><><>

The ghosts followed Charli from the third-floor to her bedroom.

"Andre, we have to find that key," Dominique said. "That turret might have clues as to who murdered Louise. If we solve the murder and bring Charli and Travis together, we will be assured of going to the good place." She folded her arms across her chest as she hovered by the ceiling. "If only we'd completed our first mission, Louise might still be alive." She sniffed back tears. "Our selfishness sent us back to ...." She bowed her head. "I cannot say the word."

"The past is over and done with, ma cherie. We *will* complete this new mission. Come, let us go to Beliveau and see how Travis is feeling."

<><><>

Travis lowered himself onto the leather sofa in front of the fireplace in his study and gestured to Max, who'd stepped into the room, to pour himself a drink and join him. Max, his dad's child-hood friend, had always been more of a father to Travis and his brother than their real dad. Max settled in the leather chair next to Travis and sipped his whiskey.

Flames licked the hearth, the crackling sounds a balm to Travis's unsettled soul. He turned to Max. "Fontaine couldn't find anyone willing to talk about Louise."

"If they know who she was having affairs with, they're not saying."

"Bloody hell. People are hiding things." Travis gave a bitter laugh. "One of her lovers is her killer. I feel sure of it."

Memories he'd rather forget crowded into Travis's mind. Two years ago, he and Louise had married. They'd fallen into bed together within hours of meeting. Louise was wild, uncontrollable, untamed. Brought up among women deemed proper by British society, Louise was unlike any woman Travis had ever met. She fascinated and intrigued him. At her urging, he bought Beliveau Manor. After several months, his lust for her had cooled. He'd recognized Louise might be mentally ill. When he told her they were finished, she'd become hysterical, declaring she was pregnant. He did the right thing and married her. There was no baby. She'd made his life a living hell.

Someone murdered her.

He tossed back his drink, as if he could wash away her lies, her serial adultery. "I need another drink." He walked to the sideboard and poured himself more whiskey. Too troubled to sit, he paced the room, done in shades of brown and beige and lined with books. He stopped before a wide table where a stack of art books rested. Placing his hand on the stack, he took soothing breaths. The books reminded him of his chosen profession, of a reputation he'd carefully cultivated, a life he loved.

"The police may have cleared me, but I feel suspicion from the people every time I go into the village," Travis said, turning toward Max.

His attention on the fire, Max spoke softly. "That's your imagination. I've not heard anyone mention suspicion of you. You took this break from work because you pushed yourself too hard after the divorce. You feel you can't relax until the killer is found, but you need to. You're not responsible for her murder." Max twisted to look at Travis. "Maybe you should take a trip to London to see your father."

"He only wants to hear from me if I go home with my tail between my legs and beg for a spot in the company."

"Hubert Gardner is a good man. He loves you and your brother, but finds it difficult to show his love. His own father drove him hard, and his mother was largely absent. I'm lucky my parents, wealthy as they were, showered me with love and let me pursue my own dreams, even if those dreams didn't sit well with them."

"If Dad loves me, he has a funny way of expressing it." Travis strode to the sofa and sank down. "I want Louise's killer found and I want to know if Jeanne truly died of a heart attack. Their deaths were so close, it seems more than conspicuous. I don't like the idea of a murderer roaming the countryside either." He slammed his glass onto the table in front of him. Whiskey sloshed over the sides onto the wood surface. "I wonder if the police are watching me, waiting for me to trip up, that they think I somehow orchestrated the murder from Australia."

"Inactivity has made you paranoid, but I admit for a small-town force to arrest a member of the prominent Gardner family for murder would be quite the feat. I think they've realized you had nothing to do with her murder. The police will get the killer. Have faith. Let's talk about something more pleasant. What do you make of our new neighbor? Charlotte bears a strong likeness to Louise."

Charli's expressive face, like a delicate and rare painting, pushed into Travis's mind. Outwardly she resembled Louise, but the similarities stopped there. He recognized a wholesomeness and kindness in Charli he'd never seen in Louise. Charli's expressive eyes held warmth and trust, two traits Travis hadn't much experience with in his life.

"The resemblance is purely on the surface," he said. "Charli is too American, too open. In some ways she's more beautiful than Louise." He picked up his glass and tossed back his drink. "I'd have to be crazy to take up with another Deveraux."

# CHAPTER EIGHT

*D*ominique and Andre zapped from Beliveau to Deveraux and settled on the roof of the house, Angel by their side.

Dominique chewed her lip, then turned to her husband. "Things are not going well. Travis is bitter, and Charli is distrustful of men. Both are stubborn. We will never bring them together."

"Don't despair. I have an idea."

"It had better be good."

He leaned over and kissed her. "I am always good."

The housecleaners were scrubbing the kitchen, the last room, when the doorbell rang. Charli, in the study poring over papers the estate lawyer had sent, went to answer. A middle-aged man, his skin browned by too much time in the sun, removed his Jeff cap and gave her a toothy grin.

"Yes?"

"Mam'selle Deveraux?"

"Oui."

He handed her a bottle of wine and a white envelope with her name scrolled across it.

"Please to give a response," he said in halting English.

She blinked, then found her voice. "Thank you. I'll be right back." She wanted to ask him in, to show politeness, but she didn't know him. Smiling, she gently closed the door and left him standing outside.

Charli ran to the study and set the wine on the desk, then examined the envelope. The ivory vellum screamed money. Frowning, she plucked the letter opener off the desk and slit the envelope open. She pulled out a folded sheet of paper in the same vellum and read the message, thankfully in English, the script flowing and feminine.

*Mademoiselle Deveraux:*

*We are your neighbors, Adele and Édouard Cantrell, who live on the other side of the village. We are anxious to meet you and your friend and show you our hospitality. We would like to invite you both to dinner tonight at our home. We will send a car for you at seven. Please let our man know if you can join us. If you are otherwise engaged, we will set another date. We hope to see you tonight.*

*Adele and Édouard Cantrell*

Charli reread the invitation. Dinner with the neighbors held more excitement than the casual dinner she and Shannon had planned. She might learn more about the area, her relatives, and her intriguing other neighbor, Travis Gardner. She hurried to give the messenger their acceptance.

She opened the door to the Cantrells' man standing where she'd left him. "*D'accord.* Okay."

"Oui."

As Charli closed the door after him, she felt a slight breeze on her neck. Again, the sensation of being watched made her shiver.

CHAPTER NINE

*A*t seven that night, a black late model Peugeot rolled up to the driveway at Deveraux Manor. Charli and Shannon, waiting by the door, rushed out. The driver, the same man who'd delivered the invitation, exited the vehicle and held the back door open for the women.

Closing the door, and without a word, he returned to the driver's seat and put the car in drive.

Charli exchanged glances with Shannon. Despite her curiosity about her neighbors, apprehension had plagued her since receiving the invitation. They didn't know these neighbors.

Shannon leaned closer. "This is so cool. I feel like a celebrity."

"I'm glad you didn't mind I accepted for us. I figured you needed a break from work."

"You can interrupt me any time for a chauffeured car ride and a fancy dinner at a French chateau. I'm looking forward to meeting the Cantrells." Shannon leaned her head on the back of the seat. "I had no idea I'd be spending so much time working while here. I thought we had that client ready to bite, but he's been a tad more demanding than we'd thought. I may have to go to London to close the deal."

"If that's what you have to do, go for it. I can handle things here while you're gone." Charli placed her hand over Shannon's on the seat. "I'm glad you're here. Thanks for coming with me. You're good moral support." She grinned. "Even if you've been forcing me out of my comfort zone for years."

Shannon laughed. "That's what friends are for, to make you uncomfortable."

After a short drive to the other side of the village, through lush rolling hills dotted with stone houses, they arrived at a three-story brick McMansion, jarring in its newness.

This part of France was steeped in tradition. Charli wondered if the Cantrells were *nouveau riche*, and not part of the old-money families, like the Deverauxes. Guilty over her cattiness, she shoved the thought aside and allowed the driver to help her from the car.

They headed up the steps as the front door, painted red, opened. An older man, wearing a charcoal gray suit, stood at the top.

"A butler or our host?" Shannon whispered.

"Madame and Monsieur are waiting," he said in heavily-accented English when they'd reached him.

Not our host, Charli thought.

He led them through a living room furnished opulently with gold brocade drapes and heavy furniture. They walked over thick ancient-looking Oriental carpets to dark wood double doors. The butler opened the doors and gestured for them to enter.

Charli had to stop herself from gaping at the wonder of all the books and artwork in the cavernous room. She could happily lose herself here. Perhaps the Cantrells were from old money after all.

A thirty-something couple rose from leather chairs facing a fireplace in which a fire crackled and burned. Smiling, they approached Charli and Shannon.

Tall, slender, with thick auburn hair curling over her shoulders, sharp cheekbones, and golden cat eyes, Adele Cantrell could grace the covers of top fashion magazines.

Édouard, taller than his wife, with dark hair and deep-set brown eyes, chiseled features, and broad shoulders reminded Charli of the heroes of the historical romance novels she loved.

"Bonsoir," Adele said. "Welcome to our home." Her English was impeccable, her accent lyrical.

"Bonjour," Édouard echoed. His deep voice rumbled through the room. He scanned Charli and Shannon, appreciation in his gaze.

"I am Adele, and this is my husband Édouard."

"Thank you for inviting us. I'm Charli Deveraux and this is Shannon Kosta."

"Happy to meet you," Shannon said. "Thanks for inviting us.

A frown creased Édouard's brow. "Charli?"

"Short for Charlotte."

"Ah. You Americans." He smiled. "We wanted to meet you although we understand you are planning to sell Deveraux Manor."

"Yes. It would be too hard and too expensive for me to keep it." Charli sighed. "It's beautiful, though."

"Perhaps when you find how good the people here are, you'll change your mind."

Charli laughed softly. "Maybe."

Adele, who'd been quiet, studied Charli through narrowed eyes. "Yes, you are a Deveraux. You bear a striking resemblance to Louise. I hope you are not in the habit of stealing other women's men, as she was."

Édouard put his hand on his wife's arm. "Darling, our neighbors don't want to hear gossip." He smiled at Charli. "Louise's death has been upsetting for all of us. We fear there is a killer wandering the area."

Charli's stomach tightened at Adele's accusation against her relative. "Although I didn't know Louise, I'm sorry about her death, and I'm sure it's been disturbing to everyone here."

"But, of course," Adele said. Although her voice softened, her eyes remained hard.

Charli noticed the exquisite pearl and diamond necklace nestled in Adele's deep cleavage, exposed by the low-cut blouse she wore.

"What an unusual necklace, Adele," Charli said. "It looks remarkably like one I saw Jeanne Deveraux wear in a photo."

Adele's eyes widened and she rubbed a long, slim, manicured finger over the diamond pendant. "Édouard gave me this recently for our anniversary. He had it made by a jeweler in Paris. I'd long admired Jeanne's but I didn't want one exactly like hers. There are slight differences between mine and the one Jeanne wore."

"Jeanne was kind enough to give us a picture of the necklace to take to the jeweler," Édouard said.

"How good of Jeanne. From what I hear, she was a kind person," Charli said.

"She was that." Édouard gestured toward the fire where a table was set with drinks and appetizers. "Let us enjoy drinks and get acquainted. Our chef is preparing something special. I was a chef in Paris at one time, but I didn't want to cook tonight and miss spending time with our lovely new neighbor and her equally lovely friend."

<><><>

Three hours later, after a meal that contained Charli's entire caloric allotment for the next two months, she and Shannon rode in the Peugeot back to Deveraux Manor.

"That food was so good, I may never eat again because nothing will ever compare to it," Charli said. "I've never had chicken so tender. And vegetables cooked so perfectly."

"It was amazing," Shannon said.

Charli hung her purse and jacket on the hat rack in the foyer when they got into the house. "I liked Édouard, but Adele was a bit of a cold fish."

"I liked him too. He and Adele don't seem especially close. She sure didn't like Louise. Regardless of whether or not you knew Louise, it was rude of Adele to say that about your relative."

"It was."

Shannon stifled a yawn. "I'll turn in. I have an early conference call tomorrow."

The women went to their bedrooms. Charli, not as sleepy as she thought, changed into pajamas and a robe and sat at the window seat in the bedroom. The drapes were open, and she gazed out over the moonlit back lawn and expansive garden, overgrown now from neglect. Louise's body was found there, dead flowers a metaphor for a dead body. Icy fingers trailed over Charli's spine.

Thinking of Louise brought Travis to mind. Although he'd been mentioned only once during dinner, he'd been in her thoughts. He was their neighbor, too. Adele had called him an angry recluse. Édouard had changed the subject.

Travis could be curt and a trifle arrogant, but the vulnerability Charli glimpsed in his eyes told her he had deeper facets than what appeared on the surface. She'd like to peel away his layers and find the real Travis underneath. Startled by that surprising thought, she sat straighter.

A pounding at her bedroom door roused her from her musings.

"Charli," Shannon shouted from the other side. "We have a problem. Our water is gone. All of it."

<><><>

"You did good, mon amour." Dominique perched on the edge of Charli's dresser. "Now, we need Travis to fall in line."

CARA MARSI

Andre lounged on the bed, petting Angel sleeping next to him. "No worry. We will nudge him."

Dominique clapped her hands. "What fun! I haven't enjoyed myself so much since that wild birthday party on the yacht with Coco."

"That woman could party." Andre sighed. "Those were the days. These young people now are boring."

Dominique sobered. "We will be careful this time and keep our focus on the mission. We will not be granted another chance to escape the…the holding place."

# CHAPTER TEN

*C*harli stood in her bedroom early the next morning and raked frustrated fingers through her hair, untangling some of the strands. It had been too late to call anyone last night. She didn't know any plumbers in the area. Surely, Travis would know someone. She punched in his number, relieved they'd exchanged cell phone numbers that day in the village.

He answered immediately.

"Travis, it's Charli. Thank God I got you."

"What's wrong, Charli?"

"The manor has no water. Is Beliveau okay? I thought it might be a water main break."

"My house is fine. I left there five minutes ago. I'm on the road now, driving to a small consulting job south of here. I'll be back later tonight. I'll call Max and ask him to send a plumber to your place. He'll let you know once he's contacted someone."

"Thank you."

"That's what neighbors are for, Charli."

Despite the water emergency, his warmth and caring calmed her. They said their goodbyes and she disconnected the call.

By late afternoon, the plumber Max called hadn't arrived. Charli paced the living room.

"Coffee?" Shannon came into the room and handed Charli a mug of the steaming drink. "Thank God Belanger put that case of bottled water in the pantry. At least we could brush our teeth and make coffee."

Sipping her coffee, Charli went to the windows for the hundredth time to look out, hoping the plumber would show up. Shaking her head, she turned to Shannon. "Max called hours ago to say he'd arranged for someone to come today."

"He also cautioned since this was a last-minute job, we might have a long wait."

"I know. I'm edgy."

Shannon tilted her head toward the window. "I hear a motor. Maybe it's him, or her."

The women parted the drapes to see a truck rumble up the drive, a late-model Ford pickup. They stared at the truck, then at each other.

"That is so not what I expected here in Normandy," Charli said.

"Maybe not the truck, but he sure is. This place corners the market on hunky men."

Charli followed Shannon's gaze to the thirtyish guy who alighted from the truck. Long dark hair curled gently around a face that looked like it was sculpted by Michelangelo. Tall, with an athlete's lean, taut body, he wore tight jeans that clung to his muscled thighs, and a white T-shirt that showcased his abs. He vibrated sex appeal.

His long-legged gait took him to their door in seconds. At the knock, Charli hurried to answer.

The man's bright blue eyes lit when he saw her. His gaze made a leisurely sweep over her, stopping at her chest before continuing down her body and back up. She shifted in embarrassment. Like any red-blooded woman, she enjoyed a good-looking guy's attention, although she didn't like being undressed with a man's eyes, as this one was doing.

"Mam'selle Deveraux?"

"Oui. Parlez vous anglais?" God, she hoped he spoke English.

He smiled, showing even white teeth against his tanned face. "Yes, I do. I am Baptiste Riviere. Max sent me."

She released a breath. "Thank you for coming on such short notice, Monsieur Riviere. Come in."

"Please call me Baptiste."

Shannon came into the foyer, a flirtatious smile on her face. "Hi, I'm Shannon."

He scanned Shannon with his piercing blue eyes, eyes Charli suspected missed nothing. "I am Baptiste." He turned to Charli. "You have no water?"

She put her hands on her hips. "Everything was fine until last night."

"I will check. It must be in your line, as no one in the area is having a problem."

"Thanks." She hoped whatever caused the water shortage could be fixed quickly.

<><><>

"Non, non. Is Travis crazy?" Dominique paced the foyer. "Why did he hire Baptiste? Can he not know he was one of Louise's lovers? Your plan to stop the water might drive Charli to Baptiste."

"Settle down. It will all work out. Charli is too smart to fall for such a womanizer as the plumber."

"You and your optimism. You said it would be safe to drive that car so fast. And now look at us."

"The car, and I, could handle the speed." Andre shrugged. "We'd be dead now anyway."

"But not when we were so young." She skimmed her hand down her dress. "I do not want to go back to that cold place."

He held out his hand to her. "Come, let's follow Baptiste while he searches for the reason for the water loss."

<><><>

Forty-five slow minutes passed while Charli and Shannon waited for Baptiste to finish his inspection. Sitting at the kitchen peninsula, Shannon worked on her laptop, while Charli, too keyed up to relax, drummed her fingers on the granite.

Baptiste came into the room. Both women stood.

"What did you find?" Charli asked.

"It is a big job."

Anxiety formed a lump in Charli's chest. "Give me the bad news."

"There is a leak in the main pipe leading to the house. Water is seeping through the grass about fifty meters in the back."

Deflated, Charli leaned against the counter. "Does this sort of thing happen often around here?"

"Non. It is most unusual."

"Can it be fixed?"

He grinned. "But of course. I am the best plumber in Normandy. I need to bring in my crew to dig around the pipe and repair it."

"How long will all that take?" Shannon asked.

"A few days."

"Few days!" Charli wanted to sink into the floor. "I need to complete our inspection of this place and catalogue the items I think are valuable. But we can't stay here with no water."

Shannon touched Charli's arm. "It's a temporary setback. Max said Travis offered his place if we had to leave."

"I'll call Max." She turned to Baptiste. "We'll be at Beliveau while you're working. I'll give you the keys to this place and my phone number."

His eyes turned to frost. "You will go to Gardner's?"

"He's our nearest neighbor," Charli said. "We can walk there."

Baptiste gave a Gallic shrug.

"I don't have a lot of money, Baptiste. Do you have any idea of what this will cost?"

"Not yet. I assure you, I am fair. I will call you later with an estimate."

"Thanks."

After talking with Max and confirming they would stay at Beliveau while their plumbing was repaired, Shannon and Charli packed overnight bags. Baptiste promised to return early the next morning with his crew. Worry accompanied Charli on the short walk to Beliveau.

Max opened the door to their knock and gestured for them to enter. "Travis isn't home yet, but I'll show you to your rooms."

"We're grateful to you and Travis." Disappointment settled over Charli. She'd hoped to see Travis. Nothing could come of her attraction to him. They lived an ocean apart.

After very welcome showers and a light supper prepared by the same elderly woman they'd met the first time they'd stayed there, whose name they learned was Hortense, Charli sat in her room, restless, unable to sleep. They hadn't seen Travis. The job he had south of here must be taking longer than expected.

An hour passed, in which the quiet of the old house upped her uneasiness. She'd glimpsed a library earlier. A book would take her mind off the plumbing woes and her confusion about Travis. She hoped she could find a book in English. She'd left Deveraux Manor in a hurry and forgot her Kindle. Walking softly, she made her way downstairs. A dim light illuminated the wood paneling and bookshelves in the study. A fire blazed in the hearth. Frightening to think of a fire untended.

She entered the library and walked to the nearest bookshelf. In the act of reaching for a thriller, thankfully in English, by a well-known writer, she froze. Soft breathing told her she wasn't alone.

CHAPTER ELEVEN

*C*harli whirled around. Travis sat in a leather club chair before the fire. He held a cut crystal glass containing a small amount of caramel-colored liquid. Whiskey, she assumed.

"Oh, sorry. I didn't know anyone was in here," she said.

"You always sneak around someone's house?" He didn't turn around.

She put a hand on her hip. "I beg your pardon. I'm not sneaking around. I'm looking for something to read. While I appreciate your invitation to stay here, I can't say the same for your attitude."

"No matter. Choose a book and go."

Despite his words, something in his voice and the way he sat here in the dark, alone, tugged at Charli's heart. She plopped down on the arm of the sofa next to him. "I don't get you. You were unfriendly the first time we met. In the village the other day, you graciously offered your cleaning crew, and you helped with my bags. Today, you sent a plumber to fix our water problems. Now, you're growling at me. Seriously, you need to figure out what you want to be."

He gaped at her before he burst out laughing. "You Americans, always so honest."

"So, what's it gonna be? Rude Travis or Neighborly Travis?"

He laughed again and tossed back his drink. "Would you like a drink?"

On the verge of declining, she thought, *what the heck.* "Sure."

Pushing up from his chair, he strolled to the sideboard and lifted the decanter to pour a splash of whiskey into two glasses. She admired the way his jeans hugged his tight butt. The man had it going on, but he needed to work on his personality.

"Make yourself comfortable," he said, handing her a glass.

Taking the glass, she sank onto the sofa and took a sip of her drink, choking as the strong liquor burned a trail down her throat.

"Are you okay?" he asked.

"I will be," she managed.

His green eyes lit with humor. "Not a whiskey drinker, I see."

"I prefer wine."

"Of course, you do."

"What does that mean? We are in France, after all."

"It appears I've stuck my foot in it, again. I apologize for my rudeness."

She took another tentative sip. It went down more smoothly and she didn't choke. "You're forgiven. This time."

He laughed again. "How are you enjoying France?"

"It's beautiful here, but I don't like all the rain. My grandparents never spoke of their homeland, and I wonder why."

He sipped his drink before answering. "Many people want to start a new life somewhere and may have bad memories of the place they came from."

"That makes sense." She ran a finger over the rim of her glass. "I read about your ex-wife, my relative. What a terrible thing to happen to her. I know you were divorced, but I'm sorry."

A shadow came over his eyes and his features tightened. "You are very simpatico, Charli."

"I try to be."

"Tell me about Charlotte, or should I say Charli, Deveraux," he said. The smoldering intensity of his eyes told her he really wanted to know her. Warmth spread through her.

"There's not much to tell." She tilted her glass, watching the amber liquid swirl, then met his eyes again. "I'm an ordinary American working woman."

"Who inherited an estate in France. You are far from ordinary, Charli."

The way he said her name, filled with raw emotion and need, made her insides shake.

"What is your life like in Philadelphia?" he asked.

"How do you know…of course, you checked me out."

"As you checked me out."

"Touché."

He laughed.

She lifted her glass in a salute. "I'm glad you find me so entertaining."

"I find you charming and unique."

She set her drink on the small table in front of her. This man drove her crazy. Part of her wanted to walk away and never see him again. Another part wanted to know all about him, to find the real Travis behind the cultured, handsome façade.

"Tell me a little about you," she said. "I know you're from London, but what made you settle here in Normandy?"

Surprise flashed across his face. "I don't get many people asking that question."

"I wonder why not?"

He grinned. "Perhaps because only an American would think to ask it."

"Are you gonna answer?" She didn't know from where she got her new boldness, but she liked it.

"My father is in London. Enough reason for me to be here."

His honesty tugged at her heart. "You don't like your dad?"

He shrugged. "He's my father. As such, I love him, but he's never forgiven me for choosing art over the family business. Growing up, he was too busy with the company to be there much for my brother and me. Max took over the father role for us."

Travis might put on the façade of not caring about his father, but the sadness in his voice told a different story.

His features softened. "Max is like a father to me."

Charli settled more comfortably, needing him to talk. A surprising sense of wanting to comfort him built in her. "What about your mother?"

"She traveled through Europe and America most of the time I was growing up. I didn't see much of her. She and Dad divorced when my brother and I were teens. Mum is married to some Polish prince now and lives in Spain. She sends us gifts every Christmas." His voice had grown bitter. "We don't hear from her on our birthdays. She's probably forgotten the dates."

"I'm sorry. I had the best, most loving parents. They died much too early. I miss them."

"Don't feel sorry for me, Charli. I survived. But it hasn't made me a trusting person."

She stood, compelled to go to him and hug him to her, to comfort him. She took a step toward him and stopped, knowing he wouldn't want her pity.

He stood, too, plunked his glass on the table, and closed the short distance between them. Inches apart, he reached out to brush his knuckles against her cheek.

"You were lucky to have such parents," he said. "They taught you empathy and love. It's no wonder you're so sweet."

The tenderness in his eyes chased away her pity. Desire surged through her and awareness tingled low in her abdomen. She drank in his scent of sandalwood. Her body swayed toward him. Fear reared up. Turning, she darted from the room.

<><><>

His thoughts chaotic, Travis seized the fireplace poker to absently stoke the dying embers before settling into his chair again. He'd let down his guard and scared Charli. Attraction burned hot and heavy between them. He'd been with many beautiful women, but none had incited the longing, and the need to protect, Charli provoked in him. And that scared him to death.

CHAPTER TWELVE

"What if Travis really did kill his ex-wife? Just sayin'." Shannon bit into her croissant and slid a glance to Hortense working at the stove.

Although Charli and Shannon didn't believe Hortense understood much English, they spoke in whispers while having breakfast the next morning.

Charli leaned across the table. "Stop that. He's not a murderer. You watch too much TV."

Hortense left the room, and Shannon met Charli's gaze. "Now that she's gone, finish what you started to tell me about meeting Travis in the library last night."

Almost as if it had a mind of its own, Charli's hand touched her cheek where Travis had brushed her with his knuckles. "He was rude at first, but we had a drink together, and I liked him. He asked me about myself and seemed genuinely interested." She looked down at the table and back to Shannon. "I told him I'm sorry about Louise. He was gracious, but I saw shadows in his eyes."

"Wonder what that was about?"

"He was married to her. It can't be easy that someone you were once close to was murdered."

"True." Shannon poured coffee into her mug from the carafe on the table.

"He also shared a little about himself when I asked."

"Do tell."

"Apparently his dad doesn't share Travis's enthusiasm for art. Both his parents were too busy for Travis and his brother when they were growing up. But they had Max, his dad's friend, and a father figure to them."

"Poor Travis and his brother. Good for Max."

"Bonjour."

Both women jumped at the deep voice from the doorway. Travis stood there, his hair damp as if he'd recently stepped out of the shower. Dressed in a black sweater that stretched across his broad chest, and wearing faded jeans that clung to his long legs, his rugged sensuality stole Charli's breath.

She hoped he hadn't heard their conversation.

"You are very serious today," he said, looking from one woman to the other. "Is all okay?"

"Even though Deveraux has no water, we were thinking of going back there to work," Charli said. She and Shannon had discussed that before they went down for breakfast. "I have to catalogue what items I want to keep and what I want to sell. This water diversion is cutting into my time."

Travis plucked an empty mug from the table and filled it with coffee, stirring cream into it. "I know you have work to do, but why not take this break to see more of Normandy? Have you been to the beaches yet where the Allies landed on D-Day?"

"No," Charli said. "We hoped we could visit once we finished at the manor."

"I'll drive you there today," he said. "It'll be good for you to take time off."

The women exchanged glances. Charli turned to Travis. "Okay. We'll do the tourist thing today. We can't leave without seeing the beaches."

He smiled. "We leave within the hour." Mug in hand, he exited the kitchen.

"Are you okay to go?" Charli asked Shannon. "No work? I have plenty to do back at the house, yet the beaches are a shrine and I want to see them."

"My staff is working on an updated proposal for that client we're trying to snag, so I can take a little break. And you might be in Baptiste's way if you go to Deveraux." Shannon grinned. "You have no water to flush toilets. You going to walk back here every time you need to go?"

"You have a point."

True to his word, an hour later, they piled into Travis's Mercedes for the ride to Omaha Beach, where U.S. troops landed in June, 1944, the anniversary of which was a week ago. In the area around the famous site, waves of tourists poured out of buses, another invasion.

Charli stuck her cold hands into the pockets of her jacket as she and Shannon followed Travis down the steps to the beach, walking carefully across the sand. Charli was glad she'd worn boots. The wind whipped around them, churning the channel.

"It's June, for God's sake." Shivering, Shannon wrapped her arms around herself. "Why is it so cold? And where is the sun? I understand better why the Allies had to postpone the invasion due to inclement weather."

Travis laughed.

Charli glanced at him. He should laugh more often. Warm and deep, his laugh was at odds with his gruff exterior. It would be too bad if Louise's murder stopped his joy. He could have a naturally morose disposition, but she didn't think so.

He twisted to look at them. "This is Normandy, where the

sun is absent most days, where it rains all year. We get hot days in the summer, but nothing like your sweltering temperatures in Philadelphia. Our winters are mild. This season has been cooler than normal. The weather reminds me of England."

"I would think after living in England, you'd want to settle somewhere warm," Charli said. "Like the south of France."

"Normandy suits me."

Without another word, he led them to a set of three sculptures jutting from the sand. The modern aluminum monuments reached for the sky, simple and majestic.

"This is *Les Braves*, in honor of all who died here." Travis's sober voice thickened, resonating with respect.

The singing of the American National Anthem wafted over them. Charli looked toward a group of tourists standing on the steps. They were led in song by a tall man who appeared to be their guide.

"Tour guides from the ships make it a practice to lead the Americans, Brits, and Canadians in their national anthems," Travis said.

"Cool." Charli swallowed around the lump in her throat and lifted her gaze to the memorial in front of her. Her eyes filled as she pictured the brave men who'd died on these beaches.

Beside her, Shannon was quiet as she stared at the sculpture.

"Very moving, isn't it?" Travis said.

Charli nodded and blinked back tears.

"I'll take you to the beaches where the Canadians and British landed," he said.

Charli met his gaze. "You must be as proud as we Americans at what the Allies achieved that day."

"I am."

"We owe that generation so much," Charli said. "My grandfather was still in his teens when he left for America. I doubt he fought in the war."

"Near the end, even the old men and young boys joined the fight. So many of the younger men had died."

Her throat thick, Charli looked again at the sculpture.

Silent, Travis turned and walked away. The women scrambled to catch up with his long-legged strides.

# CHAPTER THIRTEEN

*C*harli dawdled over her coffee the next morning. Shannon had eaten, and retired to her room to work on her laptop. Max had stopped in earlier and grabbed a mug of coffee, then left to attend to business.

While she couldn't tamp down her excitement at being so close to Travis, Charli cautioned herself to tread carefully. She couldn't fall for him. She'd leave France soon. Nothing could ever happen between them.

If she were the type to hook up, she could enjoy Travis while here. Unfortunately, or not, she wanted something lasting. She'd never had casual sex with any man. She and Tim had had a good relationship, she'd thought. But that had turned out to be a sham. Yet, in the back of her mind, she'd always known something was missing between them.

Baptiste had called her cell phone earlier to say he expected to finish their plumbing job tomorrow. He'd called the day before with his estimate, and it wasn't as high as she'd feared. She could use her credit card and recoup the money when she sold the estate.

She and Shannon could go back to Deveraux Manor, and

maybe she wouldn't have to spend more time with Travis. Soon, she'd leave the chateau in the hands of Jeanne's attorney to sell. A surprising shock of sadness hit her at the thought of never seeing the manor house or Travis again.

Heavy footsteps came toward the kitchen. Charli's pulse ratcheted up a few notches, and she steeled herself to face Travis. She wasn't afraid of him, but of the effect he had on her. When he was around, she had the overpowering urge to touch his smooth skin, to run her fingers through his black hair, to make him smile and laugh, to smooth away his worry lines. The thought froze her. In all the years she'd been with Tim, she'd never felt that way about him.

"I didn't know anyone was here," Travis said when he came into the room.

Charli smiled to hide her nervousness. "Relaxing over coffee after the great meal Hortense served. I want to thank you again for letting us stay here, and for taking us to see the beaches. And for that amazing dinner at that quaint restaurant. Your stories about adjusting to life here kept us amused."

He saluted her. "I'm glad I could entertain you."

"I heard from the plumber, and we should be able to move back to my place tomorrow and be out of your hair."

She wondered if she imagined the shadow that passed over his eyes.

"It hasn't been a problem having you here." He helped himself to coffee and sat across from her. He stirred cream in his drink, then sipped, watching her over the rim. Setting down his cup, he met her gaze. "I want to apologize again for my earlier rudeness. I've been pretty much of a recluse since…since I came back from my last job. Traveling all over the world and being away for months at a time takes its toll." He released an audible sigh. "Louise's murder has hit me harder than I'd expected. We may have divorced, but to be murdered." He shook his head. "No one deserves that."

Anger flashed across his face. "I also don't like the idea of a murderer nearby. The police are working very slowly to find the killer." He leaned back in his chair. "I probably watch too many crime shows and movies. The police in those stories always find the killer right away."

"They have to wrap it up in a short time."

"Let's talk about something more pleasant. Have you had a chance to explore the area and the land you own?" he asked. "I figured you'd want to see it before you leave."

"I plan to check it all out, but I'm trying to get things done to sell the estate. This plumbing problem has cost me valuable time. I need to get back to Philadelphia and my job. I have a one-month leave."

She touched his hand across the table. "Not that I haven't enjoyed being here, and seeing the beaches."

He looked as if he wanted to say something before his eyes shuttered. "I'll show you around today. Where is Shannon? She can join us if she's not busy."

"Thank you. I'll ask her but she's working. She's a vice-president at a graphic arts company and is under a deadline. She took yesterday off, but now it's back to work."

Forty-five minutes later, Charli waited for Travis at the front door. Shannon declined to join them. Charli shivered in the cool air drifting through the foyer, and pulled her jacket closer. Good thing she'd checked the weather before coming, or she'd be wearing summer clothes, good for Philadelphia, not so much for Normandy.

Travis appeared, dressed in a black leather jacket that looked soft and expensive. With his hair curling around his ears, the dark stubble on his jaw, his black T-shirt, his worn jeans, and black boots, he looked like every woman's bad boy fantasy. A bad boy with a heart and vulnerability. Dangerous combination.

His green gaze skimmed her. "You look nice."

"Thanks." She'd worn dark-washed skinny jeans, black ankle

boots, a deep red sweater, and her gray puffer jacket. She liked the outfit, but she also wanted to look appealing for Travis.

Uncomfortable under his scrutiny, Charli pulled her sunglasses from her pocket and slipped them on. "The sun may be weak today, but at least we have sun and it's not raining."

He chuckled. "The day is young. The rain will come. Shall we go?"

"Lead the way."

They walked side-by-side toward Deveraux Manor. When they were in sight of her house, Travis led her up a steep dirt path that wound behind the chateau. Although the heels on her boots were low, Charli had a hard time traversing the uneven ground.

She stumbled, and Travis held out his hand to her. "Take my hand. The going will be rougher until we get to the ruins."

Charli could take care of herself, yet his warm flesh and his big, rough hand enfolding hers made her feel protected in ways she hadn't experienced since walking with her dad when she was a child. Instinctively, she wanted to pull away. But she liked the heat and contentment his touch generated.

They'd traveled uphill about a half mile to reach the majestic ruins of the medieval tower. Charli stopped and stared at the tower thrusting into the cloudless blue sky, a sentry guarding all around it.

"Wow! It's more impressive close up. I saw pictures of the ruined castle, and I knew I had to see it before I left France."

Travis tugged on her hand. "Come. We'll sit in the old courtyard."

They walked over the remains of the limestone buildings half buried in the soil. Parts of the castle adhered to the tower, with other ruins spread over the hill.

Breathing heavily from the climb, Charli sank onto a limestone block embedded in the hillside. Below spread the village of Deveraux and Deveraux Manor.

Travis sat next to her and swept out his hand. "At one time all of this, including the village and where my house now stands, belonged to the noble Deveraux family."

"Magnificent. It's more glorious than the pictures let on." A soft breeze dusted the air with the scent of flowers. Peace settled over her. She could almost imagine the spirits of long-departed Deverauxes surrounding her. "I wonder why my grandparents wanted to leave all this."

"The war took its toll on Europe. Many wanted to escape to a new life."

"$\mathcal{I}$ have always loved it here." Dominique and Andre settled onto a limestone block across from Charli and Travis and gazed out over the valley. "Remember how we used to come up here and make love?"

"How could I forget? You were a tigress in bed, no matter where the bed was located."

Dominque skimmed fingers down her husband's face. "I had a lover who inspired me. I love touching you again."

Andre took her hand and planted a kiss on her palm. "God's angel was generous to grant us this ability. If we are successful in our mission, we will touch each other for eternity."

"We shocked our families and the villagers with our behavior when we lived," Dominique said.

He laughed. "Especially as we weren't yet married."

"We lived life to the fullest."

"Even though our lives didn't last long."

"We must help Charli and Travis find the passion and love they possess for each other, but don't yet know it," Dominique said. "Charli cannot leave. She must stay."

"I will think of something."

"You are so clever." She pulled her husband close and placed a tender kiss on his lips.

Cradled in Andre's arms, Dominique settled back and watched the other couple, their protégés, and their mission.

<><><>

"When was the castle built?" Charli asked Travis.

"Around 1200."

"You said the Deveraux were nobility? I never heard any of that from my dad or grandfather. I asked my dad about them and France once, but he said his father didn't ever talk about the country he'd emigrated from."

Travis fixed her with his intense gaze. "Your grandfather, François, was Jeanne's youngest brother. They were estranged. I've heard rumors of what caused their falling-out, but no one knows the truth. Jeanne didn't like to share family secrets. Perhaps you can discover it while you're here."

"I'd love to know my family history, but I'll be leaving soon and I won't be back."

Travis looked out over the expanse. "There's much here to love. Perhaps you'll change your mind."

She picked at a blade of grass peeking from a crack in the limestone. "This isn't my home. My friends and work are in Philadelphia. It's my home, the place where I was born and raised, where I'm comfortable."

"Sometimes it's good to get out of your comfort zone."

"That's what Shannon tells me. She pulls me out of my comfort zone whenever she can." Charli lifted her gaze to find Travis watching her. He'd sounded sorry she'd leave. It had taken her a year to get over Tim Sheehan and his lies. She wouldn't allow another man to influence her. She would do what she deemed necessary for herself.

"It is beautiful here." Across the valley, a stately house

appeared to shimmer on the horizon. Acres of vineyards behind the house stretched as far as she could see. Charli shaded her eyes to get a better look. "Is that the Cantrell house and vineyards? Theirs is the only modern-looking house around here."

Beside her, Travis stiffened. "You know them?"

Frowning, she turned back to him. "Shannon and I had dinner at their place the other night. They wanted to welcome us to the village."

Travis's eyes hardened. "Be careful around them."

She quirked an eyebrow. "I admit I got some disturbing vibes from Adele. Why do you say that? What do you know?"

"It is not important, not anymore."

When he didn't offer any additional explanation, she stood and brushed her hands down the sides of her jeans. "I guess we'd better head back. It's getting late." She looked around. "Are there any more ruins?"

He stood too and brushed hands down his jeans. "This is all that's left."

Charli turned to start down the path. Her foot caught in a root. Seconds later, she face-planted into the dirt.

"Are you okay?" Travis knelt next to her and gently turned her over.

Sputtering, she brushed away the grit.

He tried to help her up, but when she put weight on her right foot, she let out a sharp screech as excruciating pain shot up her leg.

"My ankle hurts so bad." She sank onto the ground.

"Let me see it." Travis squatted down and tugged off her boot. His long fingers felt her ankle, making her cry out in pain.

"I think you twisted it," he said. "I'll lift you."

As if she weighed nothing, he scooped her into his arms, with one arm under her knees and the other behind her back. He cradled her firmly against his chest. He bent at the knees and snatched up her boot, then handed it to her. Secure in his embrace, she almost welcomed the throb in her ankle.

"You can't carry me all the way back to your place. You'll fall and hurt yourself."

"Don't worry. You aren't that heavy."

He walked slowly, holding her like a precious flower ready to blow away in the breeze. If she weren't in pain, she'd laugh at the image of her as a precious anything.

The ghosts floated behind them. Dominique punched Andre in the arm.

"What was that for?" He rubbed his arm.

"A twisted ankle. That's it? Your plan? That won't keep her in France."

"She'll get to stay longer at Beliveau Manor. They will grow closer. Trust me."

Dominique flared her nostrils. "The last time I trusted you, we wrapped our car around a tree." She shuddered. "Then we spent decades in that cold place."

## CHAPTER FIFTEEN

$\mathcal{T}$he doctor summoned to Beliveau proclaimed Charli's ankle sprained and ordered her to rest it for several days with an ankle brace and alternating heat and ice packs. Charli asserted she and Shannon would be fine at Deveraux Manor now that they had running water again, but Travis insisted they stay at Beliveau until she was able to put weight on her ankle. He argued that Max, Hortense, and he were there to help so caring for Charli wouldn't fall solely on Shannon. Charli acknowledged she didn't want to burden Shannon, but she hated to be treated like an invalid. She was a healthy young woman used to taking care of herself. Her arguments fell on deaf ears.

Nothing she said swayed Travis. She stayed. Part of her thrilled she'd spend more time with him. Part of her worried she was losing valuable time. Her month leave would rapidly be over. Did she need to go back to a job she hated? The thought warred with her responsible nature. She owed it to her company to be back when she'd planned. Or did she?

Her head threatened to explode with unanswered questions.

That evening, Shannon and Charli sat on upholstered chairs in the spacious guest room Charli used. Shannon had moved a third chair over so Charli could elevate her leg. Travis was closeted in his office with some man he didn't introduce who'd shown up after dinner. The man had sharp eyes that seemed to assess everything as he'd swept his gaze over the women.

Charli released a sigh. "It's generous of Travis to invite us to stay here, but I don't like being dependent on anyone. That guy holed up in Travis's office gave me chills."

"He was unfriendly, that's for sure," Shannon said. "Maybe he doesn't speak English." She touched Charli's arm. "Settle down and let others take care of you for a change. I think Mr. Hottie Travis wants to keep you around a little longer."

"Don't be silly."

"I've seen the way he looks at you. I think he's got a thing for you."

"No, he doesn't. I look like Louise. Maybe he's still in love with her and I remind him of her."

"He likes you, Charli Deveraux. Quit making up things to worry about. You worry too much. Always have." Shannon folded her legs under her and pulled her laptop closer. "When you told me about your grandfather and Jeanne being estranged, I wanted to see if there's anything online about the family feud. Now's a good time."

Anxiety tightened Charli's chest. "I'm curious, but sometimes it's better to leave things alone. I might find something disturbing."

"Your grandfather left France a long time ago. Anything alarming wouldn't be relevant now."

Wincing at the sudden pain, Charli settled her leg more comfortably. The doctor had given her painkillers, but she wasn't due to take another one for an hour. "I did a quick online search of Deveraux Manor and the Deveraux family when Monsieur Belanger contacted me, but everything happened so fast, I didn't have time to do something more thorough. There wasn't much online anyway, mostly pictures of the house and ruins. I was still reeling with the news I inherited an estate in France, from relatives I didn't know about. I had to expedite a passport, which was beyond stressful, and apply for my leave from work. Good thing it's a slow time at the bank, so I was able to get a leave to come here. As it was, I still had to work long hours to train the associate who would fill in for me."

Shannon flexed her fingers over the keyboard. "Get out your translator app. We're gonna check French websites. They may have the dirt on your family an American site wouldn't." She typed for a while, then sat back, her eyes wide. "Wow! Here. Look." She turned the laptop to make it easier for Charli to see the screen. "I can read the names Jeanne and François Deveraux under this picture. Don't need to translate that."

Charli leaned in to study the black and white photo of a beautiful young woman who might have been in her late teens standing in front of Deveraux Manor with a boy of about ten. "That's Jeanne and my grandfather? I only knew him as an older man. He's so young, and handsome."

"Yup. Strong family resemblance. You look like them."

Charli had the same coloring as her grandfather and his sister, dark hair and light eyes. She rubbed a hand down her face. An only child, with parents who were only children, Charli grew up without an extended family of aunts, uncles, and cousins. Despite having loving parents and grandparents, she'd always felt incomplete, as if a part of her was missing. She swallowed her regret. Crying over the past did no good.

She settled back and slowly moved her leg into a more comfortable position. "Here's my translator. What does the article say?"

Using the translator app and the phone's camera, Shannon scanned the article, then read the English version on the phone screen. "Some interesting stuff here." She peered at the screen. "Here's the gist of it. Your grandfather François was nineteen when he emigrated to the U.S. Before leaving France, he married a seventeen-year-old village girl, your grandmother, Gabrielle, who was a maid at the manor house. Jeanne objected to the marriage, saying his teenage wife wasn't worthy of a Deveraux."

"No wonder François left. Such snobbery. My grandmother was the sweetest, kindest person. I was a child when she died, but I still miss her."

Shannon scanned more and read. "Here's the best part. Jeanne accused Gabrielle of stealing a valuable ruby necklace that had been in the Deveraux family for hundreds of years. That's why François left."

Charli folded her arms across her chest. "Now we know why Jeanne and François were estranged. If my grandmother had a ruby necklace, I never saw it."

"Let me read the next page. OMG. Look."

Color photos of two necklaces jumped off the screen, one a round ruby pendant, about several carats and surrounded by diamonds, suspended on a diamond chain. The other was a pear-shaped diamond pendant hanging from a pearl chain.

Charli touched the photo. "That's the pearl and diamond necklace in that portrait of Jeanne."

<><><>

"Mon Dieu! We must help Charli solve the mystery of the necklaces." Dominique lounged on Charli's bed, Angel purring next to her. "We never saw the ruby necklace the first time we left the holding place to come here and save Louise. Jeanne wore the other all the time." She put her head down. "We wasted the chance He gave us."

Andre, perched on the edge of the dresser, shook his head. "Too many lies and mysteries over the years."

Dominique sat straighter. "I thought the sprained ankle would bring Charli and Travis closer. But he is with that odd little man in his office."

"Give Charli and Travis time. I will go see what Travis and that man are discussing." Andre disappeared.

<><><>

Charli shivered and grabbed the blanket from the arm of her chair.

"You're cold?" Shannon asked.

"Lately, out of nowhere, I feel air blowing over me."

"Ooh, sounds spooky."

"Nothing spooky about it." Charli hadn't told Shannon about the white cat on her bed. There was no such thing as ghosts.

# CHAPTER SIXTEEN

Travis saw Fontaine out and returned to his study. Glass of cognac in hand, he sat at his desk. Frustrated with the slowness of the local police, Travis had hired a private detective to find Louise's murderer. For Jeanne's sake, as well as Louise's, he wanted the perpetrator found. The detective had brought news.

The police kept some details of Louise's death from the public. He knew the police sometimes held back facts of a crime to trip up the killer. All they would reveal was she'd been strangled and they'd found her body in the garden of Deveraux Manor. There'd been no jewelry or other personal effects on her at the time.

Through his connections, Fontaine had obtained a copy of the police report. Louise had either fallen or been knocked down and hit her head on a rock before being strangled. Louise had used Travis, lied to him, and was a serial cheater, but he never wanted her to suffer such an agonizing death. He felt sorry for her, had for a long time before she died.

One thing Fontaine told him had him reeling and reaching for the cognac.

Louise was pregnant when she died. Two lives lost, one an innocent. He and Louise had stopped being intimate over a year before she died. She'd tried to seduce him back to her bed, but he'd lost all feeling for her. Another man had gotten her pregnant, and now she and the baby were dead.

He tossed back his drink and threw the glass into the fire in the hearth. It hit the flames and shattered. Like his life, thrown into chaos when Louise entered it with her constant demands and disruptions.

He strode to the sideboard for another cognac. A draft of air, light and cool, brushed the back of his neck. He whirled around, sure someone was in the room with him. Emptiness faced him. Maybe he didn't need that drink after all.

Determined to escape with some mindless TV in his room, Travis strode out of the study and headed for the stairs, taking them two at a time. He passed Charli's room and heard women's voices. He smiled, glad Charli could relax after all she'd gone through lately. She'd insisted on going back to Deveraux. He wanted to be sure she had care, so he'd convinced her to stay at Beliveau a little longer. Truth be told, he liked having her near.

In his suite, he shut the door behind him and sank onto the loveseat in the sitting area. He'd been drawn to Charli from the moment he'd met her. Outwardly, she favored Louise, but he sensed goodness in Charli that was missing from Louise's troubled soul.

Charli made him feel whole again, ready to take on the world. His heart and soul craved the openness and honesty she possessed. She'd leave soon to go back to Philadelphia. Regret tugged at his chest.

Travis grabbed the TV remote and willed his thoughts from Charlotte Deveraux.

<><><>

"What did you find?" Dominique had joined Andre in the study.

"Louise was pregnant when she was killed."

"Mon Dieu! Whose baby?"

He shrugged. "If only we hadn't been called back to the holding place when she was murdered, we would know who the murderer is, and perhaps the father of her baby. I suspect they are one and the same."

"Poor Travis. He wanted children. Remember how Louise fooled him into marrying her, saying she was pregnant?"

"If Travis discovers the father of Louise's baby, he might discover her killer."

<><><>

The next morning, Travis snapped his briefcase shut, plucked his duffel off the floor, and started out of the study. He had a small job at the mansion of a billionaire south of Paris. Although he was taking a break from the major jobs that kept him away for months at a time, he liked to keep busy.

He went into the foyer as Charli came gingerly down the stairs, helped by Shannon. Travis set down his bags and offered Charli a hand.

She smiled her thanks, and immediately his mood lightened. He took her hand in his, relishing the warmth of her flesh.

Charli's eyes swept to his bags and back to him. "You're leaving?"

"A private job near Paris. I'd contracted for it several weeks ago. I'll be back in three days."

"Oh, well, we might be back at Deveraux Manor by tomorrow. I'm feeling better. Thanks again for inviting us to stay here."

She dropped her hand from his, leaving him deprived of her touch. Could he be so desperate he imagined regret on her face when he'd said he was leaving?

"Thanks for letting us stay," Shannon echoed.

"You're my neighbors. Of course, I'd help."

The doorbell rang. Travis strode to the door and opened it to Baptiste Riviere. He and the muscular plumber stared at each other. Travis clenched his jaw, fighting the urge to punch the smirk off the other man's face.

"What do you want, Riviere?" he asked.

"I have come to give Mam'selle Deveraux the key to her house," Riviere answered. "My crew has finished."

"Max called on you to repair the plumbing? You have nerve showing up here."

Riviere laughed without answering and looked past Travis.

"Mam'selle." Riviere held out the keys to Charli.

Shannon took them from him and gave the plumber a friendly smile.

Travis inhaled a deep breath, seeing the image of Baptiste and Louise having sex in Beliveau's sunroom. He'd thrown the man out of his house then, and he wanted to now.

"Thank you, Baptiste," Charli said. "How much do I owe you?"

"Here is the bill." He handed it to Shannon. "Pay when you can."

"Thanks for helping," Charli said.

With a dip of his head to the women, Baptiste left.

Travis turned to them. "Charli, I'm glad you're feeling better. If you need anything else, call Max or me. I must be on my way."

"See you later, Travis," the women said in unison.

Travis found Max in the garage preparing the car for the drive to the train station. "Max, why did you hire Riviere? I told you to call Hugo."

"Hugo was busy and the women needed help right away."

"Don't call Riviere for anything. I don't care if my house is flooded."

"Sorry, Travis. I know your history with him, but he's a good plumber, and I wanted to help the women."

"I know you did. Didn't mean to jump on you. Let's go. I can't miss the train."

## CHAPTER SEVENTEEN

*A*fter Travis left, the ghosts followed Charli and Shannon into the kitchen. Dominique sat at the table with the women.

"Mon amour." Dominique raised her head to her husband, hovering by the ceiling as Hortense prepared breakfast. "This plan of yours is not working. Charli and Travis are not together."

He inhaled. "Ah, that food smells heavenly."

"We won't be heavenly unless we complete our mission."

"Trust me, ma cherie."

<><><>

After lunch, Shannon and Charli settled into the Mercedes for the ride back to Deveraux Manor with Max. Charli still hobbled on her ankle, but felt much better, and she no longer needed the brace.

When they started out, Charli, in the front passenger seat, turned to Max. "Would it be too much trouble for you to take us into the village first? We haven't much food left at the house."

"No problem."

He drove to the village, where he found a parking spot near the square. He helped Charli from the car, then held out his arm for her to slip her hand through. With him on one side and Shannon cupping her elbow on the other, Charli negotiated the narrow sidewalks. Villagers stared as they passed. Charli grinned at the sight they must make—a middle-aged man escorting two young women, one of whom limped, and who was also heir to the largest estate in the area.

"I'll help you select the best food for the best price," Max said. "I can bargain with these shop owners. When they see foreigners, they automatically hike up the prices."

"Appreciate it," Charli said. "I got the impression the first time I was here that the shopkeepers tend to take advantage of the tourists. I'm not good at bargaining in English, and certainly not with my pathetic French."

They went into the patisserie where she'd shopped before and bought fresh-baked baguettes and macarons. Next, the meat market for filet mignon, and the seafood market for succulent fish caught that morning. The outdoor greengrocer was last.

The colorful array of fruit and produce—apples, oranges, lemons, peppers, tomatoes, made Charli salivate. "I want one of each."

"Me, too," Shannon said.

As with the other shops, Max negotiated with the owner, at times the exchanges becoming heated. Maybe she should ask Max to come into the village every time she and Shannon needed something.

Or, Travis might agree to accompany them when he got back from his trip. Warmth speared her at the thought of spending more time with him, of getting to know him, of unmasking the softness she'd glimpsed in him.

Shopping over, Shannon and Max carried the bags to the car. Charli, walking slowly, held onto Max's arm.

"Charli!"

She turned at the deep male voice. Édouard Cantrell, holding a tote with baguettes peeking out, strode toward them.

"Hello, Édouard," she said.

"Hello," Shannon said, a smile in her voice.

Max stiffened, but said nothing.

Édouard lowered his gaze to Charli's foot, which she held up from the ground. "You hurt yourself?"

"Sprained my ankle. I'll be fine."

"May I see you home?"

"Thank you, but Max is driving us."

Édouard bowed slightly. "I am always available if you need anything."

"Thank you."

With a cool smile, he turned away and entered one of the shops.

Charli looked up at Max. "I get the feeling you don't like Édouard much. He and his wife had us for dinner. He seems okay."

Max shrugged. "I try not to listen to gossip, but I hear things. Rumors only. Don't worry yourself."

Once back at the manor, Shannon put away the groceries while Charli rested in the sunroom, a cup of tea on the table in front of her.

Max's reaction to Édouard had surprised her. Undercurrents simmered below the tranquil surface of the tiny village. There was also the obvious dislike Travis held for Baptiste.

She loved a good mystery and wanted some answers, but the cautious part of her warned to stay out of it. Nothing that happened here was any of her business. Her priority was to prepare the house and grounds to sell. Heaviness settled in her chest. Although she'd always be a Deveraux, this dignified old house with its ruins and rolling hills, in her family for centuries, would no longer belong to a Deveraux. She wished she could afford to keep the property and still live in Philadelphia, but she didn't have the income to keep homes in two countries.

Once she sold it, her connection to her new-found heritage would go. Her entire life she'd hungered for a place where she had deep roots. This house and village would always be in her heart, if not her life. She rubbed her temples to ward off the headache forming.

The photos of the ruby necklace and the pearl and diamond one flashed into her mind. She couldn't leave until she found them, or knew what happened to them. She wondered if her grandmother had stolen the ruby one, as Jeanne accused. Maybe her grandparents sold it to help them get established in their new life in America.

"Charli?"

She looked up to find Shannon in the doorway. "What's up?"

"Something strange."

Charli sat straighter. "What do you mean?"

"I opened one of my dresser drawers and it looked like someone had gone through it. I opened a few other drawers and they looked the same."

"Was anything taken?"

"I didn't notice. I'm wearing the little jewelry I brought with me, and I took my phone and laptop to Beliveau. There was nothing of value to steal."

"Baptiste was here alone for days. If he did it, why would he make it so obvious?" Chills skittered up her spine. "What could whoever it was possibly be looking for?"

# CHAPTER EIGHTEEN

*S*hannon and Charli stood in Shannon's bedroom after they searched the room for any missing objects. "Someone sure did go through your room. I might be less scared if something was taken."

Shannon sank onto the bed. "How so?"

"If things were stolen, we could write this off as a common thief. It looks like whoever did it was searching for something specific."

"And if he didn't find it, he'll be back."

"Exactly what frightens me. Let's check my room and the rest of the house."

Charli's dresser drawers and closet had been rifled. Anger mingled with her fears. She narrowed her eyes at Shannon. "If it's Baptiste, he has a lot to answer for. Since whoever came in here didn't try to hide what he did, I wonder if it could be Baptiste. He'd be the prime suspect, so why would he make it obvious? I think we should call him back to the house today and ask him."

"I want to punch him in the gut if it's him, but maybe we shouldn't be alone with him, just as a precaution." Shannon's eyes widened. "I hope he didn't make a duplicate of the key."

"God, I hadn't thought of that. Don't get ahead of yourself." Charli blew an errant strand of hair away from her face. "Let's go to the tower, in case the intruder found a way to open the door."

"And if he did, we'll never know what valuables he stole."

With Shannon's help, Charli made it to the third floor. She leaned against the wall, catching her breath.

Shannon rattled the door handle hard, but, as before, it wouldn't budge. She started to turn away and froze, then ran her fingers over the old-fashioned brass lock. "These scratches weren't here before. Someone tried to pry this open." She moved aside to let Charli have a look.

"You're right. Maybe whatever the intruder was looking for is in the turret room at the top."

"You need to rest. Tomorrow we'll go through every room in this house, every desk drawer, every place someone could hide a key."

<><><>

The ghost couple, along with Angel, watched the women.

"Think, Andre, where could that key be?" Dominique said. "Jeanne always kept it with her, so where did it go after she died?"

"I am thinking, love."

She touched his arm. "It's time we revealed ourselves to Charli."

"Non. We do not want to frighten her to death. And we do not want to lose any more of our essence."

"Louise and Jeanne saw us that last time we were here."

He shook his head. "Louise tried to use us for revenge on her romantic rivals, and we frightened Jeanne so much, we never appeared to her again. We lost some essence for nothing. Then we were called back. We cannot take any chances. Charli is an innocent and deserves peace. Angel showed herself and caused Charli to become hysterical."

Dominique tapped a finger to the corner of her mouth. "We should not have appeared to Louise and Jeanne, but we must appear to Charli. I will prepare her first, and I know just the thing."

<><><>

Charli's ankle felt well enough for her to accompany Shannon on a search for the tower key the next day. They'd already gone through the bedrooms and the few rooms on the third floor. Charli made a list of the items they'd found in the various room, items she thought had value. The search of the main level, which contained the living room, sunroom, study, and kitchen was taking longer. Her frequent rest breaks slowed them, and after a while, they gave up, resolving to continue later.

Clouds gathered in the sky as afternoon bled into evening. They sat at the kitchen peninsula nursing glasses of burgundy wine.

"I'm exhausted," Shannon said.

"Same here. We've gone through a lot of the house and found no key." Charli swallowed some wine, hoping the warm slide of the rich liquid down her throat could calm her. "What was the intruder looking for?"

"Let's go into the village and talk to Baptiste. We shouldn't suspect him unless we have some proof. If he can't be trusted, why did Max hire him?"

"Good point. Although Travis doesn't seem to like Baptiste."

"I'm sure Max would send over the best person for our plumbing job." Shannon glanced at Charli's foot. "You can't walk into the village with that ankle. Why don't we ask Max to drive us to Baptiste's office tomorrow? We'll have a witness in case Baptiste incriminates himself."

"I suppose Travis is still away."

Shannon's lips formed a teasing grin. "You want to spend time with hottie Travis?"

"He's okay." A slow burn started at Charli's neck and spread to her face.

"You are full of it, girlfriend. You have the hots for our sexy neighbor. Even if he's been rude."

"He did us a favor by letting us stay at his place. And he's been helpful with the cleaning people. He's actually quite nice."

"Okay. Someone is smitten."

Worried she might reveal her growing closeness to Travis, Charli said, "I need more of this wine. Glad I stopped the painkillers yesterday." As she reached for the wine bottle in front of her, her hand brushed her empty glass. The glass fell to the floor and shattered.

Frowning, Charli raised her gaze to Shannon's. "Odd. I barely touched it."

"I'll clean it and get you another glass."

"Sit. You did more work than I did today." Charli stood and took a step. Her foot tangled in the leg of the stool and she sprawled on the floor.

Shannon jumped up. "Did you cut yourself?"

"No, I'm fine. What's this?"

"What's what?"

"There's a piece of paper sticking out from under the refrigerator." She stretched, but couldn't reach it.

"I'll get it." Shannon helped Charli stand, then took her arm to guide her back to her stool. Once Charli was settled, Shannon bent to pull out the paper and handed it to Charli.

Charli skimmed it. "An old newspaper clipping. What the hell?"

"We can read it together, but first I'll clean up and get you another glass. I don't want you hurting yourself seeing as how you're suddenly accident prone."

Shannon grabbed the small brush and dustpan hanging on

the wall and swept up the glass shards. She pulled a goblet from the cabinet, sat next to Charli, poured two wines and slid one to the other woman.

Charli spread the paper in front of them. "It's dated June 12, 1933. The story is in French. Damn, my French is bad."

"Use your translator app."

"Good idea." Charli pointed to the clipping. "We don't need a translation for this picture."

The grainy black and white photo captured a young couple, late twenties, or early thirties, standing by a low-slung sports car. The woman's hair was light, probably blonde, cut in a short bob popular with stylish women of the time. Dressed in a flowing dress with a flower design, she smiled brightly. Her companion had close-cropped dark hair, and he wore pleated pants and a tennis sweater. He faced the camera with an arrogant smile. The woman held a large white cat.

Charli's breath hitched. The long-haired cat looked like the one who'd appeared, then disappeared, on her bed. She dismissed that thought. Most long-haired white cats looked alike.

"Wow, what a beautiful couple."

Shannon's words brought Charli back to reality. A draft of air ruffled her hair and tickled her neck. She looked up at the ceiling.

"What is it?" Shannon asked.

"Did you feel that air?"

"No."

"Probably my imagination." Charli blinked and studied the photo again. The cat wasn't the same as the one in her dream. Of course, it wasn't. "I wonder who these people are." She read the caption under the picture. "Andre and Dominique Deveraux."

"Your relatives?" Shannon asked. "I met your parents once. Except for the clothes and hair, Andre looks exactly like your dad."

The women read the article with the help of the translator app. Swallowing around the lump in her throat, Charli turned to

Shannon. "So sad what happened to them. Andre was my grand-father's brother. No wonder he looks like my dad."

Sorrow clutched at Charli's heart. "My dad would have loved seeing this picture, seeing all of this." She missed her dad, and her mom. Both died while Charli was a junior at art college, her mom from cancer, and her dad from a car accident shortly after. Charli always believed her dad really died of a broken heart. Not wanting to think about the two people she'd loved the most in the world, she pushed aside her grief.

She shivered as another whisper of air brushed her neck. She reread the translated article on her phone again, in case she missed something.

"Andre and Dominique Deveraux, both thirty-years-old, were killed instantly when their sports car hit a tree," she read out loud. "Speed is suspected as the cause of the accident." There was more, a brief history of the Deveraux family, and of Dominique's equally noble family, but she didn't bother rereading that. "Their cat, Angel, was in the car with them. She perished in the crash too."

"Sad for all of them. You seem awfully upset about something that happened long ago."

"My dad died in a car crash too."

Shannon reached out and patted Charli's arm. "I know. I'm sorry."

Charli shook herself as if she could shake away the pain of memories. "I need to tell you something. Remember that dream I had about a cat? It was so real."

"That was the night you screamed."

"Yes. That cat looked like the one in this picture."

"You're scaring me. Are you saying you think you saw a cat ghost?"

Charli rubbed a hand down her face. "No. My imagination is overactive. I don't believe in ghosts."

<><><>

"Now, what, ma cherie?" Andre asked his wife. The two sat on stools at the peninsula as Charli and Shannon talked. Dominique reached across and ran a finger over the paper. "We were so beautiful. And young." Wistfulness filled her voice.

"Others envied us. Especially Maurice."

Dominique squeezed her husband's hand. "Your brother's envy of our love and our lifestyle may have turned him to murder."

"With me gone, more of the Deveraux fortune was his."

"And he squandered it on his gambling habit."

"All that is left is this house, some of the land, and the necklaces, if they haven't disappeared forever." Andre shook himself and gazed at his wife. "We cannot blame Maurice for all of it. I didn't appreciate my heritage while I lived. Our selfishness paved the way for Maurice to waste the Deveraux fortune and sent us to the holding place. This is our last chance to make things right and earn our redemption."

"We will show Charli ghosts do exist. It is the only way."

# CHAPTER NINETEEN

*S*hannon and Charli stood outside Deveraux Manor early the next morning waiting for Max to pick them up for the trip into the village.

Charli lifted her face toward the sky, inviting the sun's warmth. "I can't believe today is so pleasant after that rain last night."

"Me either, and it's warm enough to only need a sweater."

"At least we won't have to fight the weather when we see Baptiste."

"It was really nice of Max to agree to drive us."

Travis's black Mercedes wound up the drive and stopped before the house. Travis exited the car and opened the passenger door for the women.

"Travis, I didn't expect you. I thought Max was driving us. That you were still away." Happiness colored Charli's voice. She wanted to treat Travis as no more than a neighbor, but the pounding in her heart told a different story.

Shading his eyes from the sun, he smiled at them. "I got home late last night. I'm free today and thought I'd drive you."

Like a woman starved, she filled her eyes with him. A lock of his dark hair, ruffled by the breeze, fell over his forehead. Charli's fingers twitched with the urge to touch his hair to see if it was as soft as it appeared. She wondered if the light stubble on his jaw would rub her face when they kissed. Her insides heated.

The women walked the few feet to the car. Shannon jumped into the back seat. "Charli, you sit in front with Travis. With both of us in the back, it looks like he's our chauffeur and not our friend."

Shannon's sly smile provoked a glare from Charli. Shannon laughed.

Travis helped Charli into the front passenger seat. She clicked on her seatbelt while he rounded the hood and got into the driver's side.

"Thanks for driving us today," Charli said as he pulled out onto the road. "Ordinarily I'd walk, but I need to be careful until this ankle is back to normal."

He glanced over at her. "Are you still in pain?"

"I'm much better. The pain isn't anything a few aspirin can't handle. And I can almost walk normally."

"Where do you want to go in the village?" he asked.

"To see Baptiste," Charli answered. "We called his office and the person who answered said Baptiste would be in all morning. We didn't want to put off talking to him."

Frowning, Travis stole a quick glimpse at Charli. "You are going to see Baptiste? Why?"

Charli released a breath and clasped her hands on her lap. "While we were at your place, someone went through our things, like they were looking for something. Baptiste was in there for several days working. We're not accusing him, but we want to ask him if he knows anything about it."

Travis swore softly under his breath. "It's good you called Max and me. You shouldn't be alone with that man. No woman should."

"Why?" Shannon asked.

"He's a womanizer. I'll accompany you when you talk to him."

"I appreciate the offer, but---."

"We were hoping you'd say that," Shannon piped up before Charli could tell Travis she could handle Baptiste by herself.

Charli looked straight ahead. Her parents had taught her independence. She'd never had to rely on a man, except her dad when she was little. She didn't want to start now.

They parked behind Baptiste's truck, which was in front of his small street-level office on one of the side streets, and alighted from the car. Travis helped Charli over the uneven sidewalk and through the door to the office. A startled Baptiste rose from his desk when they entered.

He smiled. "Welcome, mam'selles. Please, have a seat." He ignored Travis and gestured toward the two chairs in front of his desk. Neither woman sat.

"We have a little problem we hope you can help with," Charli said. Travis squeezed her elbow, communicating his support.

"Is something wrong with the job I did?" Baptiste asked.

"No problem with that," Shannon said. "While we were gone, someone went through our things. It doesn't look as if anything was taken, but we don't like it."

Baptiste's blue eyes widened and he held out his palms. "I am so sorry. I have a reputation for honesty, as do my men."

Charli's ankle began to throb. "Do you have any idea who could have done this?"

Baptiste rubbed a hand over his eyes. "Non." He looked down, then back to her with a sheepish grin. "But I am responsible."

"How?" Travis asked.

"I forgot to lock the door one day when I left. Someone must have come in during the night when the place was empty. I apologize profusely if I caused you problems. For my error, I will forgive your bill. My repairs are free. Will that satisfy you?"

Charli leaned against Travis. "You left our house open. Of course, I won't pay you." She narrowed her eyes at him. "I hope you didn't make copies of the keys. If so, please let me have them." She held out her hand.

Baptiste backed away. "Non. I have nothing."

"Let's hope we have no more problems with anyone breaking in." Charli looked up at Travis. "We need to go."

They settled into the car, and Charli released a relieved sigh. She buckled her seat belt, then turned to Travis. "I'm not sure I believe him, but he sounded sincere."

"To be safe, you should change the locks. I'll send a locksmith over."

"Good idea."

"We need to be careful," Shannon said as Travis pulled out of the parking spot. "Someone was looking for something. If they didn't find it, they'll be back."

"Keep your doors and windows locked at all times." Travis drove through the narrow streets and headed out of town. "I'm a phone call away, but I'll check on you every day, and so will Max."

Charli reached out and touched his hand where it rested on the gear shift. "Thanks."

He slid a glance to her. The heat in his green eyes warmed her with promise. Promise of what? She focused on the landscape rolling by and tried to ignore the excitement sweeping through her.

A thought took her from her sensual musings. "Travis, have you ever been in the tower and turret at Deveraux Manor?"

"No. Why do you ask?"

"The tower door is locked. I've tried all the keys Monsieur Belanger gave me and none work. I talked to him and he said he gave me all the keys he had. He didn't try to get into the tower, only put the unused couture items in storage to preserve them, but left everything else in place. I need to get in the turret room before we put the house on the market. Belanger is sending over a list of items Jeanne had assessed before she died. I need to check that against what I find in the house, all the rooms."

Charli leaned back in her seat. "My one-month leave is flying by. The bank expects me back."

"You hate that job," Shannon said. "Just quit."

"They depend on me. I can't leave them in the lurch."

Shannon leaned forward and patted Charli's shoulder. "You're a responsible person who is a tad scared of change. Take a chance now. You'll sell the house and come away with money to support yourself, or you can buy into Chloe's gallery sooner than you planned."

Charli chewed her lip. "I'm afraid."

Travis kept his attention on the road. "I agree with Shannon. Sometimes you have to leave everything and do what you want."

Charli wondered what he'd left behind. She'd think on that later. "Do you know anything about the turret room, Travis?"

"Jeanne used the room for storage, but she never let anyone in. She carried the key with her. I don't think Louise ever had it."

Shannon, in the back seat, moved closer. "It wasn't with Jeanne when...when she died?"

"When the police found her body, she had nothing on her."

"Do you know anything about a pearl and diamond necklace and a ruby one?" Charli asked.

"What do you know about the necklaces?" Surprise colored his voice.

"We saw a picture of Jeanne wearing the pearl and diamond one, but I haven't found either necklace in the house. They might be in the locked turret room."

Travis pulled up in front of Deveraux Manor and cut the engine. He twisted to meet Charli's gaze. "The diamond and pearl necklace meant a lot to Jeanne. She wore it all the time. She and Louise fought over it. Jeanne refused to give it to Louise. I never saw a ruby one."

Shannon folded her arms over the back of the car's front seat. "The police found Louise in the garden. What made them go there? Were they looking for her?"

"They received an anonymous tip," Travis said.

Feeling like she was in the middle of one of those murder mystery dinners, Charli shifted in her seat. "They found Louise's body, then they found Jeanne dead?"

"No. They found Jeanne a few days before. Louise called the paramedics to say Jeanne had collapsed in her bedroom. When the ambulance arrived, Jeanne was dead. The cause of death was ruled a heart attack. Jeanne was in her nineties and had a bad heart. It makes sense."

"No wonder Monsieur Belanger advised us to use bedrooms other than the master. I guess he figured we'd be creeped out staying in a room where someone died," Charli said. "He also told me Louise inherited the estate when Jeanne died, but with Louise gone, it went to me. I feel sorry for both of them. Could Louise have taken the pearl and diamond necklace?"

Travis pulled the keys from the ignition. "That's a good possibility. But where is the necklace now? Let's go inside. I'll secure the house before I leave and make sure the deadbolts are working."

He checked the doors and windows to make sure everything was locked tight, and instructed them to activate the deadbolts that could only be unlocked from the inside. He left, promising to call later.

Charli sat on the sofa in the study and propped her leg on the coffee table in front of her while Shannon made them hot tea.

Sipping their tea, the women were silent for several minutes. Finally, Charli set down her cup. "I find it bizarre Jeanne died a few days before Louise."

"I agree."

"I wonder if they're connected."

Shannon shuddered. "Coincidences happen."

"Let's go over what we know." Charli held up a hand and began counting off on her fingers.

"Louise is killed. Her body is found in the garden here. The authorities won't release all the details of the crime. They found Jeanne's body days before Louise's. The priceless necklace Jeanne wore all the time is missing. So is the tower key." Charli's mind a whirlwind, she picked up her teacup and sipped the relaxing brew.

Shannon counted on her fingers. "Louise must have taken the necklace before the paramedics came."

"But where is it now? There's the ruby necklace," Charli said. "Also missing, but no one is mentioning that one."

"True. And someone is searching for something in this house. Who knew we'd walk into a real-life mystery?"

Wrapping her hands around the warm cup, Charli settled back in her seat. "We're in Normandy, France. Look around this place. It's ancient. Kind of lends itself to intrigue. The turret may hold the answers to our questions."

# CHAPTER TWENTY

"*A*ndre, Charli needs to get into that room."

"Yes, ma cherie. We've looked everywhere for the key. We can assume Louise took it from Jeanne's body. Where did she hide it?"

Dominique shuddered and petted Angel sitting next to her on the roof of the manor house. "If we'd not been called back to *that* place, we might have seen Louise's murder and where she put the key."

"Had we been successful in our first mission, Louise might still be alive."

Dominique placed her hand on her husband's arm. "We must not concentrate on the *ifs*. The Big Guy has given us a second chance."

"Do you wish we'd lived longer, love? Maybe our children's grandchildren would be living at Deveraux Manor now."

"I do wish it, but we cannot change the past," Dominique said.

He looked out over the countryside. "We are together for eternity. That is what matters."

"I'm going to show myself to Charli."

"You might scare her to death, ma cherie." He took her hand in his. "You will lose more of your essence."

"I will sacrifice some of my essence. It is the only way we can help."

<><><>

Charli sat at the kitchen peninsula while Shannon hunted in the cabinets, refrigerator, and pantry for something to make for dinner.

"I wonder if any of the shops deliver food." Shannon's voice was muffled by the refrigerator as she searched it. "We can't keep going into the village every couple of days to buy groceries, especially with your bad ankle. I wish there was a supermarket nearby where we could stock up on food. We're spoiled by all the big markets at home."

Charli sipped from the bottle of water in front of her. "I imagine some of the stores deliver, but would anyone want to come here? We had enough trouble getting a cabbie to drive us out here."

"Good point." Shannon withdrew her head from the refrigerator and shut the door. "I can make us omelets. Tomorrow I'll walk into the village. We never thought to buy groceries while we were in the village this morning to see Baptiste."

The doorbell rang. The women looked at each other.

"Wonder who that is." Shannon rubbed a hand down her jeans. "I'll answer."

"Don't open the door unless you know who's there."

The sound of the front door opening, then voices, Shannon's and a male, put Charli on alert. She stared at the kitchen doorway.

A minute later Shannon walked into the room, followed by Édouard Cantrell holding a large cloth shopping bag. The requisite baguette poked from the top.

Charli wasn't sure she felt like company but Cantrell was a neighbor and he'd entertained them in his home a few days ago. She stood. "Édouard!"

"No need to get up, Charli. I don't want you to hurt your ankle."

She sat.

He held up the bag. "I have brought dinner."

"Dinner?" Shannon looked over at Charli and shrugged. "Ask, and you shall receive."

"Oui. Dinner. I miss cooking, and I don't do much of it any more. It will be my pleasure to prepare dinner for two beautiful ladies."

A sudden draft of air blew across Charli's face. She looked around, but Shannon and Édouard didn't seem to notice anything out of the ordinary.

"How nice of you," Charli said to him. "We know you must be busy. We appreciate the gesture, but we can fix our own meal. We hate to take you away from Adele."

"Adele is out of town, and I did not want to eat alone. I hoped to share dinner with my new neighbors. Enjoy the wine I've brought while I cook a meal you will never forget."

"Let us help," Charli said.

"If you insist. You can cut up the chicken and mushrooms while I prepare the sauce."

"Deal," Shannon said.

Later, satiated with the delicious meal Édouard had prepared, Charli raised her glass to him. "Wow, you were right. That meal was one of the best I've ever tasted. My compliments to the chef."

Shannon rubbed her stomach. "That chicken smothered in cream with butter and mushrooms undid years of eating healthy. But who cares?"

Édouard laughed. He'd proved to be an entertaining man, full of outrageous stories about cooking in top restaurants in Paris. They'd had fun preparing dinner together.

"I'm still laughing inside at some of your stories," Charli said. "I love the one about the guy who brought his chicken to your restaurant and wanted you to prepare a meal for it."

"That was crazy," Shannon said. "My favorite was the customer who didn't like the way her bouillabaisse was spiced and marched into the kitchen to add her own spices."

"I have many more. Maybe someday you will hear them all."

Part of Charli wanted to hear the stories, wanted to stay in this place. She had obligations in Philadelphia. Or did she? Saving that thought for another time, she said, "Adele would have loved this meal."

Édouard's lips curved in a smirk. "Adele has eaten enough of my cooking. And heard enough of my stories. She is enjoying herself in Paris with her lover."

Charli choked on the wine she'd just sipped. Shannon, sitting next to her, patted her on the back.

"Your wife is with her lover?" Charli managed when she found her voice.

"Of course. It is the French way."

"I can't believe it's everyone's way in France," Shannon said.

With a Gallic shrug, Édouard drank some of his wine. "It is the way among our set. I take lovers, too."

He fixed Charli with a calculating stare. "Louise and I were lovers. Before and after she married Gardner."

"Oo-kay." Not knowing what else to say, she poured herself more wine.

"Did Travis know?" Shannon asked. "About you and Louise."

"Like all Brits, Gardner is provincial. He couldn't accept his wife took lovers."

"I can understand that," Shannon said.

Charli needed to change the subject. "Since you, uh—knew Louise, did she ever show you the turret room here?"

"I have not been in this house in a long time." His eyes softened, and he was once again the charming dinner guest. "Louise told me about a delightful turret room at the top of the tower. I have never seen it."

"Unfortunately, we haven't either. We can't find the key to the tower which leads to the turret room."

"Have you tried to force the door open?"

"The door is too beautiful and old I don't want to damage it. We could consider taking it off its hinges, but they're so rusted I'm afraid they'd crumble and we couldn't get the door off."

"What about calling in a locksmith?"

"I will if I have to, but I'm afraid he'll wreck the antique lock and the door."

"Perhaps I can help you open it," he said.

"That would be great," Shannon said.

Shannon and Charli led the way to the third floor. Édouard examined the door and lock, jiggled the lock, then threw himself against the door, as if by strength alone, he'd open it.

His face fierce, he hit the door with his body several times, but the door held fast. He turned to them with tight lips.

Charli put up a hand. "We've tried everything, but it's hopeless."

"I will be glad to call a locksmith for you."

Suspicion rose in Charli. Édouard was too anxious to get into that room.

"Thank you," she said. "But I need to think about it."

He dipped his head. "I will be glad to give you any help you need."

Charli gave him a half smile. The front doorbell rang, making her jump. This place suddenly had more traffic than her favorite Philadelphia coffee shop.

CHAPTER TWENTY-ONE

"*I*'ll get it." Shannon headed downstairs.

"I guess we'd better go, too." With a wistful glance at the tower door, Charli hobbled toward the steps. Édouard rushed to help her.

Voices from the foyer reached them. Charli couldn't mistake Travis's deep voice with his British accent. A thrill ran over her.

Édouard released her elbow. "What is *he* doing here?"

"He's my closest neighbor," Charli said. "He's been a help to us."

"He killed Louise."

Charli shot him a narrow-eyed glare. "That's not true."

"You would take up for him? I see he's seduced you, too."

"He hasn't seduced anyone."

"He took my Louise from me."

"He married Louise." Her mind raced. Édouard, married to Adele, mourned Louise. This place had the makings of a soap opera, or *The Real Housewives of Normandy* with a deadly ending.

When they reached the entrance hall, Shannon and Travis turned toward them.

Travis stiffened when he saw Édouard. "Maybe I should come back tomorrow."

"No need to do that, Travis. Édouard was just leaving." She hated to be rude, but she had no patience for what threatened to be a testosterone display. She gave Édouard her sweetest smile. "Thank you for dinner. Would you like a drink before you leave?"

"I must go." He lifted Charli's hand and kissed it. As if a mask dropped over his face, his features relaxed. "A pleasure to spend time with two such charming ladies." He smiled at Shannon before tramping to the door. He ignored Travis on his way out.

"That one is bad news," Travis said when Édouard had closed the door behind him.

*For God's sake, did no one trust anyone around here?* Charli bit her lip to keep from saying the words out loud.

"He cooked us a meal," Shannon said. "That was good of him."

"Cantrell never gives anything without expecting something in return." Travis held up a bag much like the one Édouard had brought over. "I have the makings of dinner."

Charli leaned on the railing, favoring her ankle. "Thank you, Travis. We appreciate it, but it is kind of late now and we've eaten. I'm not sure I'll ever get used to the French way of eating dinner late. Will the food keep for tomorrow? Join us now for a glass of wine and for dinner tomorrow?"

Travis handed the bag to Shannon. "I would have been here earlier, but a client called with a question, and that took more time than I'd thought. You'll need to put this in the refrigerator. I accept your invitations for the wine now and dinner tomorrow."

"Great," Charli said.

Shannon took the bag from Travis. "Could you help Charli into the study? I'll bring wine and glasses."

Travis slid an arm around Charli's waist. "You're still in pain?"

"Not so much. I went up and down the stairs just now, and it put strain on my ankle. I need to sit." She tripped, and Travis held her tighter.

"What were you all doing upstairs?" Travis asked.

"Édouard wanted to help us open the tower door so we could get into the turret room."

"Did he?"

"Nope."

"Let's get you to a chair."

With Travis's arm encircling her waist, warmth swirled through Charli. He held her closer than necessary to help her walk. She wished the distance to the study was longer.

Travis made a fire to ward off the chill of the cool Normandy night. The three sat before the flickering flames, an opened bottle of burgundy wine on the low table in front of them. Charli was glad the cellar held enough of the cheaper wine from the village so they wouldn't be tempted to open the more valuable bottles.

Travis picked up his goblet and took a sip. "Max has arranged for a locksmith to come here tomorrow morning."

"Thank you," Charli said. "You really trust Max, don't you?"

"Max has always been there for me, since I was a child. Even when he was away for months at a time for his work, he still managed to keep in touch with me. I'm closer to him than my own father. It's the same for my brother." A shadow came over Travis's eyes and he looked away.

Shannon's phone rang. She looked down at the screen and stood. "Gotta take this call. My team has been working hard to nail that London client. Hopefully, this is good news." She connected the call and walked out of the room.

Curiosity, like the flames in the hearth, licked at Charli but she didn't feel comfortable asking Travis about Édouard's revelations concerning Louise. Maybe she could get him to talk about it though. She twisted her fingers around the stem of her glass, searching for words.

Travis tossed back his drink and poured himself another. He

held the bottle out to Charli. She shook her head, and he set the bottle on the table.

"You and Cantrell don't much like each other," she said.

He sat back and locked his eyes with hers. "There's been animosity between Cantrell and me since I came to Deveraux Village."

"Why is that? You don't have to answer if you don't want."

"I don't mind. I find you easy to talk to. Other than Max, it's been a while since I felt relaxed with anyone."

His words heated her more than the fire. When he wasn't being rude, Travis could charm the paint off a masterpiece. A little voice whispered she had to be careful not to fall under his spell. She didn't know him, yet crazy as it seemed, she felt she'd known him a long time.

"Cantrell and Louise were engaged to be married." Travis shot her a wry smile. "Then I came along."

"I thought he and Adele had been married years."

"Only eight months."

"Eight months? I got the impression it had been longer."

"Adele pursued Édouard for a long time, but he had eyes only for Louise. When I married Louise, he took up with Adele. She's a vindictive woman, and used to getting her way. She never forgave Édouard or Louise for making her his second choice."

"Why did Adele marry him? Couldn't she find someone else who loved her for herself? Or did she love him so much, she'd take him any way she could? And why is everyone around here in such a hurry to marry?"

He laughed. "We're very traditional. I doubt Adele ever loved Édouard, but she wanted his property, and she was desperate to be accepted in a place that values family ties. The Cantrells go back generations here, but they've fallen on hard times, like most of the European nobility. They owned land and a noble name, but not much else. Adele's family is nouveau riche. He needed her money. Marriages that are more like business arrangements are still the norm for some. Same with the Deveraux family at one time."

"You'd better believe that's one tradition I'm not keeping."

He laughed again, this time with real joy. His smile transformed his face, making him look younger, vulnerable, a man she could fall in love with. Charli swallowed some wine, drowning out that dangerous thought.

"Did Édouard love Louise?" she asked.

"I believe he did."

"Did she love him?"

His features tightened. "Louise loved only herself. She was a troubled soul. I felt sorry for her."

Charli had no words. The undercurrents of emotion churning around them were hot enough to peel paint.

A shadow flashed over Travis's face. He set down his half-empty glass and stood. "It's getting late and you're tired."

She pushed up from her seat. "I'll go to the door with you and set the deadbolts."

They went into the foyer together. With his hand on the doorknob, he turned to her. Something hot and wicked sparked in his eyes. She couldn't look away.

"Charli." His voice thick with need and yearning, he gripped her shoulders and pulled her to him. His lips, urgent and hungry, claimed hers. She wrapped her arms around his waist. She parted her lips, inviting his possession. Rubbing against him, she savored his perfect, muscled body. His kiss inflamed her until rational thought fled, and she knew only her intense desire to taste and feel all of him.

His lips gentled and he cupped the back of her head. "Travis," she moaned into his mouth. He tasted like wine, rich and intoxicating.

He slid his palms down her hips to cradle her buttocks. His hard erection pressed against her stomach. A slow ache built in her, a longing for something untamed.

With a low groan, he pulled away and touched his forehead to hers. Their ragged breathing was the only sound in the quiet hall. Her heart kept a rapid beat.

Finally, he held her at arms' length, his eyes intense. "I should say I'm sorry, but I'm not. I've wanted to do that since the first moment I saw you."

Charli stepped back, freeing herself from his touch. Missing his heat, she massaged her arms. "Don't you dare apologize. I wanted it too." She looked down. "I needed that."

He touched her chin with his fingers until their eyes met. "Don't ever be ashamed of your needs."

She inhaled a sharp breath, trying to summon some semblance of control. "I was hurt deeply once. It's taken me a while to get over it."

"I'm sorry, Charli. You're too good a person for anyone to hurt."

"We've both been hurt, but I suspect it's made us stronger. I know it's made me stronger. But a little less trusting." She moved away. "Thanks again for bringing dinner. We'll see you tomorrow."

His lips curved in a sexy smile and he bent to sweep her lips in a gentle kiss.

"Good night, Charli."

# CHAPTER TWENTY-TWO

*A*s promised, the locksmith arrived early the next morning. He changed the locks on the three outside doors—front, the kitchen door that led to the back of the property, and the one off the deck in the sunroom. Thankfully, he spoke English. Charli showed him the door to the tower. He examined it carefully before proclaiming the antique lock, centuries old, was part of the door. He confirmed her fear that the hinges would crumble if they tried to take them off. To open the door, he'd damage the lock and the door. Charli thanked him and said she'd continue to search for the key. Stress tightened her stomach. If she didn't find the key within a week, she'd have to call the locksmith back. Her leave was almost up, and her return tickets were non-refundable.

After lunch, Shannon stood from the peninsula and threw down her napkin. "I've got an important conference call in fifteen minutes that I need to prepare for. My poor employees. It's past six at home and they're still working hard. This client is proving more elusive than we thought. I figured we'd have him signed by now and I could chill and enjoy this trip, and help you. I'll clean up the dishes later. Do you want anything before I head up?"

"My ankle is good today so I'll be fine." After a night of erotic dreams starring Travis, Charli woke feeling better than she had in a long time. His passionate kiss might have something to do with her happy mood.

"I hate to abandon you," Shannon said.

"You're not abandoning me. I've spent the morning cataloguing items. I need a break. The sun is shining for a change and I want to get outdoors. I'm going to do some sketching today. It might be my last chance. I plan to walk out to the ruined tower."

Frowning, Shannon looked down at Charli's ankle. "I hate to be a mother hen, but are you sure you're okay to do that? Are you safe alone?"

"I'm fine. I'll wear my sneakers and take my time. If someone wants something in this house, I doubt they'd be searching through the ruins." She swept hair back from her face. "I'll make sure to lock up. Go. I know you have some things to do before the conference call."

The trek to the ruins took more effort than Charli had anticipated. Maybe she should have stayed at the manor, but seeing the elusive sun filled her with cheery anticipation and made her antsy to venture outside. Truth be told, she kept procrastinating on doing what she needed to prepare the house for sale. She had to be back to work when her leave was up, and Deveraux Manor wasn't nearly ready to put on the market. She needed a distraction from the pesky little voice that asked if she really wanted to go back to that job.

She also needed a distraction from obsessing over that kiss. No man had ever kissed her with such hunger and passion, as if he wanted to consume her. Since Tim, she'd carefully cultivated the persona of a woman content with her life, a woman who didn't need or want a man. She'd been with Tim since she was fourteen, had never really dated until they split. Her few dates had been disasters.

Kissing Travis had changed everything. She wanted one man. She wanted Travis.

The tower came into sight, majestic on its hill with the sun slanting off the weathered limestone. Charli stopped to take a breath and feast her eyes on the ruins. To think her ancestors had once lived in the castle that stood on this land. She had no fear of being alone. Instead, she felt oddly protected, as if the spirits of other Deverauxes kept watch.

Although she wore sunglasses, she shaded her eyes and let her gaze roam the countryside. The lushness of the land spoke to her. She loved Philadelphia, but she'd never had the deep connection with her hometown that she experienced looking over the swelling green hills of Deveraux. She wished her parents were here to share this with her.

Clutching her sketchbook and pencils, she trudged to a large rock that afforded her a view of the tower perfect for sketching. Inhaling the fresh air redolent with the scent of grass and wildflowers, she sat and opened her sketchbook. Her work at the bank had consumed most of her time, leaving her too exhausted to paint and sketch. She'd missed it and vowed to take more time for her art when she got back to Philadelphia.

Below, the Seine wound like a sluggish snake, brown and unhurried. A tourist ship drifted along the water. She could make out people moving on the decks or sitting in chairs to soak in the rare sunshine. Peace, like soft watercolors, washed over Charli. She'd come home.

She took out her pencils, setting them on the rock next to her. Engrossed in her drawings, Charli lost track of the time. She looked at her phone, surprised two hours had flown by. She massaged her lower back and examined the sketches, pleased with them. When she got back to Philadelphia, she'd transfer the drawings to oil on canvas. If she could find the courage, she'd ask Chloe to show them in her gallery.

Heaviness settled in her chest at the thought of leaving. She'd never see Travis again. After their first meetings, when he'd been gruff, he'd turned out to be a good neighbor, ready to help. The sadness she glimpsed in his eyes arrowed straight to her heart. He'd never experienced loving parents like she had, although he was lucky to have Max. With Travis's looks, he must have had girlfriends, but maybe he'd never felt love from any of them.

She wanted to ease his pain, to show him real love. She rubbed a hand over her eyes, as if she could scrub away that surprising thought.

"Charli!"

At her name, shouted from across the meadow, she looked over. As if she'd conjured him up, Travis walked swiftly toward her. Her insides trembled.

"Charli," he said again when he reached her.

His smile made her heart flutter.

"What are you doing out here?" he asked.

She held up her sketchbook. "The sunshine excited me so much I had to come out and draw. And I'm putting off the things I need to do at the manor. What are you doing here?"

He lowered himself to a rock next to her. "I stopped by the house and Shannon told me where you were. You're an artist?"

"I'm not sure artist is the right word. I like to draw and paint. Always have."

"May I see?" He held out his hand.

She gave him her sketchbook. He flipped the pages, perusing the drawings. Finally, he handed the book back.

"You're very talented. I take it you do contemporary art."

Delight at his compliment set her pulse to racing. "Thank you. I prefer contemporary art, but I always enjoy the Old Masters. I plan to put my sketches on canvas with oil when I get back to Philadelphia. Your praise means so much, coming from someone with your background."

"My tastes and education run to the Old Masters, but as a lover of all art, I enjoy the restorations, bringing the paintings back to life, whether classic or contemporary. Have you ever had a showing?"

"No. I'm too afraid to exhibit my paintings in public. I work part-time at a gallery, and I hope to buy my way to partner there. My friend who owns the gallery has offered to host a showing, but I keep resisting."

"Don't be afraid to share your talent with others." He reached out to brush hair back from her face, hooking strands behind her ear. His touch ignited a rush of longing in her. She should move away, but her traitorous body wanted his closeness.

Travis pulled away first. Like a cloud obscuring the sun, she missed his warmth.

"I called my friend Chloe, who has the gallery, and told her I own a Frank Stella. She was so excited she asked me to bring it home so she could show it before I sell it."

He leaned back on his elbows. "You're going to sell it? I helped Jeanne acquire it from a neighboring estate when the owner died."

"I love the painting. I love most of what he does. But I need the money it would bring."

"Why is a talented artist like you working at a bank?" he asked.

She raised an eyebrow. "You found that out online?"

He chuckled. "Guilty. Why the bank?"

"Most artists, like most writers, don't make enough to pay the bills. I have bills to pay." She plucked a blade of grass. "When I graduated from art college, I got engaged to my high school sweetheart. We'd been together since ninth grade. We were saving to buy a house and pay for a big wedding. I had to find a well-paying job." She raised her gaze to find Travis focused on her. "I was afraid if I tried to make a living at my art, I'd fail miserably."

"You're married?" Shock registered on his face. "You mentioned last night you'd been hurt. By your husband?"

"No. I never married."

"What happened, Charli?"

The gentleness in his voice urged her to tell him everything. She wrapped the blade of grass around her finger, not looking at him.

"Tim and I moved into an apartment together near the University of Pennsylvania campus after we got engaged. He had started law school at U of P. My parents died when I was in college, and I have no siblings. Tim was all I had, except for my good friends. We planned to marry after he got his law degree."

"What happened?" he asked again.

Charli stared into his eyes. "He got married, but not to me." She blinked back tears. She hated that she still hurt. "He eloped with our neighbor while he was still engaged to me."

Travis knelt in front of her and gathered her to him. "That man didn't know the treasure he had in you."

"Thanks." Her voice was muffled against his hard chest.

He tenderly pushed her away. "Do you want to talk about it?"

She nodded. "I like talking to you. Tim and I had been together so long, we were like two good friends, comfortable, but without passion. I liked it that way. My parents were very much in love. My mom died of cancer, and my dad died in a car accident a few months later. I think he wanted to die because he couldn't live without her. I don't want to ever love anyone that much."

She swiped at a tear. "Wow! I've never verbalized before that I was okay without passion. I've thought it but was afraid to say it." She skimmed a finger down Travis's cheek. "What is it about you that makes me want to bare my soul?"

He grabbed her hand and placed a gentle kiss on her palm. "We've both been hurt. Maybe our souls recognized that. I'm sorry for what he did to you, Charli. What did you mean your fiancé eloped with your neighbor?"

She laughed softly. "A young woman who attended the

university moved into our building. We'd been there almost three years, and Tim didn't have much longer before he graduated. I'd started planning the wedding. I sensed the attraction between our new neighbor and Tim, but I was complacent about our relationship so I dismissed it as my imagination. Three months later, when he told me he was going to stay with a friend for a few days to prepare for an exam, I believed him. The next day, he called me from Las Vegas with the news he'd eloped with our neighbor."

Travis sat back on his haunches. "He married her, and you knew nothing about the affair?"

"Color me dumb."

"Charli, you are not dumb. You're better off without him."

"Tim called me several times after that, but I wouldn't answer his calls. He stopped calling."

Travis pulled her to him and rubbed his hand up and down her back. She inhaled his faint scent of the outdoors and sandalwood. She linked her arms around his neck and gave herself over to his soothing arms. His heart beat sure and steady against her cheek.

# CHAPTER TWENTY-THREE

*R*eleasing her, Travis scrunched down on the rock with Charli, holding her hand. Their shoulders and thighs touched. His warmth radiated through her. She resisted the urge to melt into him.

With a contented sigh, she said, "This place is amazing. The hills, the ruins, the village, the manor house, and the Seine like a slithering snake surrounding it all. I feel a connection to this land I've never felt anywhere else. I wish my dad could have seen all this."

"Your family has lived here for hundreds of years. Their blood runs through you. You're lucky to belong to a place with such meaning. I fell in love with Normandy and this valley the first time I saw it three years ago."

Charli turned to face him. "You don't ever want to go back to England?"

His eyes shuttered. "I keep a flat in London. I go back occasionally when I have an assignment there. I see my brother and cousins. My work takes me all over the world. Some jobs can take months."

He dropped her hand and gazed toward where the Seine

meandered. A ship appeared, one of the barges that regularly plied the waterway. The peaceful setting belied the churning in Charli's stomach. Being so close to Travis ignited a yearning for something free of constraints, a desire to throw aside the caution that had marked her life, to try for the brass ring of pleasure and daring. And lasting love. She wanted to know all she could about what made Travis the man he was now.

"You never see your dad when you go back?" she asked.

"My father and I had a falling out years ago. We haven't spoken since."

"I'm sorry. I was close to my dad. I miss him."

Travis turned to her. He brushed hair back from her face. "You are lucky to have had a close relationship with both your parents."

Charli took his hand in hers, wanting to take the sadness out of his eyes. "Things haven't always been easy for you."

He shrugged. "I grew up with privilege. I can't complain. I wanted something different than my dad wanted for me."

"Does your family know about Louise, that you married her, that she died?"

"My brother knows."

"Have you tried to make amends with your dad?"

"You sound like Max and my brother. Maybe someday I can forgive my dad enough to reach out to him. But not yet."

Travis gazed out over the hills. "I was on a yacht off the coast of Australia when Louise was murdered," he said, his voice so low she had to strain to hear. "I'd been there for several months, restoring a Picasso the owner's children had thrown bowls of cereal at." He scrubbed a hand over his face.

"The world doesn't always appreciate art. Even though you were divorced, I imagine it hurts that someone you'd once cared for had died in such a terrible way."

"Yes, and I also don't like that there's a killer wandering the countryside. The police aren't working hard to find the murderer. I'll protect those who are close to me."

"The world doesn't always bend to justice, either."

Travis brought her hand to his lips. He kissed her knuckles, then released her.

Charli rubbed her arms and focused on their surroundings.

"This day is too beautiful to talk of death," he said.

"It is." Something he'd said popped into her mind and she faced him. "Wait! You said someone's children threw cereal at a Picasso? That's a sacrilege."

"That isn't even my weirdest restoration. I could write a book with some of the odd things I've seen and all the unusual reasons paintings are damaged."

"You *should* write a book."

"Someday."

Charli touched his forearm. His muscles flexed under her fingers. "How did you first come to Normandy? Vacation or work?"

Leaning on his elbows, he stared at the sky. "I came to get away after the falling out with my father. Plus, the work and the travel had taken a toll on me. I needed to recharge."

"Deveraux is a sleepy little town. I can see why it would appeal to you."

"I rented a place in the village. Then I met Louise." His voice held a tint of bitterness.

"How did you meet?"

"I was enjoying a cup of coffee at an outdoor café when Louise walked by, swinging her hips. She went into the café for coffee, then joined me at the table. I hadn't invited her, but she intrigued me. And she was hot." He turned back to Charli. "Although I've traveled the world, the people around me when I was growing up were very proper. They suppressed their feelings. Louise was so different, so free-spirited. I loved her disdain for what others thought. She fooled me, I'm ashamed to say. I should have seen her true nature."

"Don't beat yourself up over it. We've both been fooled. The important thing is we survived. Tell me more about her. It helps to talk."

He shifted and looked away. "Louise came on strong to me, and I didn't resist. I found her fun, charming, and captivating. We had a whirlwind affair. I wanted her as much as she wanted me. Beliveau Manor had been on the market for almost a year. I offered for it, at more than the asking price, and got it. She moved in with me. I don't regret buying Beliveau. It's my home now. I met Jeanne and liked her. I helped her with things around her place." He chuckled. "I ended up liking Jeanne a hell of a lot more than Louise."

Charli rested her hand on his arm. "Everything I hear about Jeanne makes me wish I'd known her."

"She was a kind person who tried to help Louise. Louise's mother died when she was a child, and she never knew who her father was." He shook his head. "That branch of the family had issues. Maurice was Jeanne's brother, and Louise's grandfather. His wife died while giving birth to Louise's mother. He never remarried. If the rumors are true, Maurice had a cruel streak. Louise shared that cruelty. I didn't recognize it at first. My relationship with her began to sour. She was easily bored, and liked to party. She resented my work. She liked her life in Paris."

"Is that why she took back up with Édouard Cantrell?"

"He was one of her many lovers." Travis said the words without resentment, but with resignation.

"You loved Louise. That had to break your heart."

"I'm not sure I ever loved her, but I thought I did. I have a lot of confidence, some might say misplaced pride, in my talent to make paintings come alive again. Maybe a little arrogance in my ability to read people. Yet, I fell for a woman who wasn't what she seemed. My ego took a hit. Our differences grew too great, and I asked her to move out."

"But you married her."

He met Charli's gaze. "She said she was pregnant. I did what I thought was the right thing. I asked her to marry me." A haunted look came into his eyes. "She wasn't pregnant."

"She lied?"

"She did."

"She wanted to marry you, despite her love of partying? I would think she wouldn't have wanted to marry anyone."

"I've asked myself why she was so desperate to marry me. I think Louise was desperate for love and stability but didn't know how to get it."

"How long were you married?"

"Not quite four months."

"You divorced her when you found out she lied?"

"Yes. Divorce is pretty simple in France. She moved back to Deveraux with Jeanne. I rarely saw her after that. Within the year, we'd divorced by mutual consent. Months later, Jeanne and Louise were dead."

Charli tilted her head back, digesting his words. Puffy clouds scudded over an indigo sky, calming her. She sat up and met his eyes. "Louise died of strangulation?"

"Yes, and something else contributed to her death. I hired a private investigator. Turns out Louise either fell or was knocked down and hit her head, then was strangled." A haunted look came into his eyes. "She was pregnant."

Charli put her hand to her mouth. "How terrible, for her and her unborn child. Can't the police do a DNA test on the fetus? That might help locate the killer."

"They did, but found no matches."

"That's too bad. Even though she cheated on you, she was still a human being with hurts and fears. She must have been terrified at the end."

Travis slid his arm around Charli's shoulders, drawing her close. "You've got a generous heart, Charli."

A cool breeze blew over them. Charli hugged herself, then stood and gathered her art materials. "It's getting chilly. I guess I'd better head back."

He stood, too. "I'll walk you and take you up on that dinner invitation." He frowned at her foot. "You walked here by yourself. You're better?"

"Much."

He held out his hands. "Nonetheless, I'll carry your things."

She handed him her supplies, and they headed back to Deveraux. Despite the chill, Charli's insides warmed. She felt closer than ever to Travis.

CHAPTER TWENTY-FOUR

*T*ravis enjoyed the camaraderie preparing dinner, coq au vin, with Shannon and Charli. While the meal cooked, they sat in the study drinking the wine he'd brought.

He'd forgotten how to have fun, to let himself go, if only for a short while. Other than his estrangement with his father, he'd had a good life before Louise, a full life. He'd always dated women who were elegant, classy, well-bred. Louise's high spirits and devil-may-care attitude enchanted him. But she'd put him through hell with her craziness, the times he'd had to go to Paris and bail her out of one trouble after another. He'd allowed her to suck out his soul.

He watched Charli now as she conversed quietly with Shannon. The flickering light from the fire in the hearth played over Charli's face, accenting her high cheekbones. Her expressive almond-shaped eyes looked out at the world with trust. He'd gravitated toward Charli from the moment he met her. She spoke to a part of him he'd lost long ago, his faith in goodness. Something about her gave him hope. She reminded him of the innocence he'd had as a young man, when he was sure his father would support him in whatever he wanted to do, when he still believed his cold mother loved him.

Lying in bed alone at night, he'd fantasized about making love with Charli, about undressing her, of kissing his way down her lush body. For the first time since the disaster his life had been with Louise, he'd begun to come alive.

Charli must have felt him watching because she turned to him. Something hot arced between them, promising passion, dreams fulfilled.

Shannon cleared her throat, disrupting his musings. She swung her attention from Charli to Travis, a knowing smile on her face. "I'll go check on the chicken in the oven. It should be done soon."

He barely heard her, his focus on Charli. He wanted to keep her close, to listen to her throaty voice with her Mid-Atlantic accent, to run his fingers through her thick dark hair. He wanted to give her only happiness, to wipe away the hurt she'd suffered by that other man's betrayal.

She looked away, cutting their connection.

"Have you spoken to a realtor yet about putting up the house?" he asked, hungry for her attention again and hopeful she'd say she didn't plan to leave for a long while.

Meeting his gaze, she sipped wine and set the glass on the low table in front of her. "Monsieur Belanger and a realtor will be here in two days to give me an estimate."

A heavy weight settled in his chest. "You will leave soon?"

"Not as soon as I'd expected. I can't put the house and grounds up for sale until I've inventoried this whole place." She ticked off on her fingers. "Jeanne might have hidden valuables, like the necklaces. I need to hire someone to assess the wine in the cellar. We've been careful not to drink the really good stuff. Belanger hasn't given me the list of Jeanne's assets yet. She'd had her possessions insured before she died. I need to know what she had and compare it to what I find. The turret room might yield a lot of treasures, if we could get into it. I'm going to have to call in a locksmith. I can't wait much longer. I wonder what it's like in there."

"It's round."

She laughed, a sexy sound that tossed aside all thoughts of locked rooms and lost keys. He wanted to hear more of Charli's laugh.

"What time is your appointment in two days with the realtor and Belanger?"

"Noon. Why?"

"I'll come over to help. You're a capable woman, but you're young, and an American. There's still much sexism in this part of France, and some anti-American attitudes. I know the value of the houses. Belanger is honest, but I suspect he's anxious to settle the estate."

"Okay. I appreciate your offer, although I've been researching home values here." She shrugged. "There's nothing like Deveraux Manor for sale."

Shannon entered the room. "Dinner is served Milady and Milord."

Travis couldn't remember when he'd had such pleasant dinner companions. Shannon and Charli kept him laughing with stories of their jobs, Philadelphia, and something called Mummers, who held a parade every New Year's Day.

"These mummers dress in outlandish costumes and strut through the streets of Philadelphia?" he asked.

"Yes," Charli said. "The most fun for the adult onlookers is going in and out of the bars while the parade is on." She laughed. "The parade isn't as much fun to watch when you're sober."

Travis threw back his head and laughed. Having dessert of macarons with coffee in the kitchen, he didn't want the evening to end.

"I just thought of something." Charli jumped up from the table. "Be right back."

She returned with a yellowed piece of paper. "We found this under the refrigerator." She spread the old newspaper clipping in front of him and leaned over him.

A musty scent wafted up from it. "What is this?"

"Do you know about Andre and Dominique Deveraux? Apparently, this Andre was my grandfather's brother."

Charli moved to sit across from him. Without her near, a chill filled the air.

He scanned the article, then looked up to find both women staring intently at him. "There is a popular legend in these parts about Andre and Dominique. Some believe they still walk among us as spirits. They were what we now call jet setters. They traveled and partied all over the world. Andre had a younger brother, Maurice. The story goes that Maurice, a bit dour, resented his older brother for appreciating life too much. Maurice took care of the household while Andre pursued other pleasures. Their mother had died years before. When their father died, he gave a larger share of his estate to his eldest child, Andre."

"Did the others inherit anything?" Charli asked.

"Maurice, Jeanne, and François each got a small amount of money. As I understand it, even though Andre owned the house and land, the others were permitted to live in the manor as long as they wanted."

"There's a lot to learn about my family," Charli said. "How do you know all that?"

Travis met Charli's inquisitive gaze. "Much of what I learned about the family is common knowledge in the village. Like the British royals, the people were obsessed with them. Still are. Some of what I know, I got from Louise."

Shannon stood. "I'm bringing over that bottle of wine and some glasses. I think we're going to need a drink while you tell us the dirty secrets about Charli's family."

Charli laughed. "Good idea." She turned back to him. "Tell me about my relatives, the good and the bad."

Travis accepted a glass of wine from Shannon. "It's not always pretty."

"Most families aren't," Charli said.

Settling back, drink in hand, Travis continued. "The story is Maurice had gambling debts. What he inherited didn't cover nearly what he owed. When Andre died, his portion, including the house and grounds, was distributed equally among the three living siblings. I understand it was a substantial sum of money and assets. Maurice squandered his on gambling."

"What happened to the money Jeanne and my grandfather inherited?" Charli asked.

Travis sipped wine before answering. "I assume your grandfather used his share to emigrate to America. Rumor has it he washed his hands of his family when he left and said he wanted nothing to do with them and wanted nothing more from them, relinquishing any future stake in the estate. They never heard from him again. Jeanne wisely invested hers. She never married, but accumulated some wealth from her investments. Maurice's debts grew, and Jeanne agreed to sell off some of the land and assets, including jewels, to help him. The necklace she wore was one she refused to part with." Travis shot Charli a wry smile. "I understand Maurice stole from Jeanne, too."

"My head is spinning." Charli leaned toward Travis. "How soon after the father died did Andre and Dominique have their fatal accident?"

"Two months."

"Did anyone think to investigate?" Shannon asked.

Travis folded his arms across his chest. "The story has taken on mythical qualities over the years. It happened in the 1930's. Since the heir to the Deveraux family died, I imagine the police conducted an investigation. I've never heard they found anything suspicious."

CHAPTER TWENTY-FIVE

*A*fter Travis left, Shannon and Charli sat before the fire in the study drinking hot tea. Relaxed and cozy, Charli folded her legs under her.

"You've got some family," Shannon said. "Secrets, money, lost jewels, and murder. Sounds like the plot of a great mystery book or a Lifetime movie."

Charli laughed. "At least they're not boring."

"That they're not."

Shannon's lips quirked in a sly smile. "You and Travis seem awfully friendly."

Charli's stomach fluttered. "He's a neighbor who's trying to be helpful."

"You keep telling yourself that, girlfriend. The way he looks at you it's obvious his thoughts where you're concerned are far from neighborly." She wagged a finger at Charli. "And you like him. A lot. Don't deny it."

"You're wrong. He's no more than a friend. That's my story, and I'm sticking to it."

"Yeah, right."

Like the dying fire before her, Charli had felt dead inside for a long time, stuck in a soulless job, reeling from betrayal and heart-break. Being with Travis made her come alive and dream that things would change for the better, that her life would again be joyous. She didn't know if she could trust him or any man yet, or if she could risk her heart breaking. But she was healing.

"It's getting late." Shannon stood. "I have an early conference call tomorrow so I'd better hit the sack."

"I'll stay here for a while and bank the fire."

"Good night."

Charli straightened her legs and leaned her head on the back of the sofa, thoughts scrambling through her mind like paint splattered against canvas. She'd enjoyed Travis's company today. He'd changed from that first day when he'd been grumpy, dark, unhappy. He smiled more now, walked with a lighter step. Her pulse ratcheted up. She hoped she had something to do with his improved mood.

The missing necklaces pushed into her mind. She had to find them or know what happened to them before she put the house on the market.

The beginnings of a headache pounded her temples.

<><><>

"I'm going into the village for some food and pastries," Shannon announced after lunch the next day.

Charli pushed up from the table and began clearing dishes. "I'll go with you. I need the fresh air. My ankle is back to normal. I can't do much more cataloguing until I get that list from Belanger."

Shannon fixed her with a teasing grin. "I would have thought you'd gotten enough fresh air yesterday with Travis."

Charli gave her a look from narrowed eyes, prompting a laugh from Shannon. "I had a pleasant time sketching. Nothing more."

"Being with Mr. Hottie didn't hurt." Shannon carried her dishes to the sink. "I kid you, but you seem happier since we got here than you have in a long time. Normandy agrees with you. I'm glad to see you enjoy yourself."

Shannon wiped her hands on a towel. "You should stay in and rest. You did a lot of walking yesterday. I'll handle the grocery shopping and even cook us dinner tonight."

"I can't refuse one of Shannon Kosta's meals."

"You do realize you're probably getting an omelet."

"So long as there are macarons for dessert. I can't get enough of them. The ones in Philly can't compare. I may take a few boxes home with me and freeze them for the long winter."

After Shannon left, Charli sat in the living room with her laptop to do further research on the local real estate market. The Deveraux land alone should bring her a pretty penny. If they found the necklaces, she'd get them appraised and sell them. A thrill shot through her. Maybe the money would give her the courage she needed to quit her bank job.

Maybe she should look for courage within herself and take a leap of faith.

The doorbell rang. Frowning, she set her laptop aside and walked to answer it.

She looked through the door's peephole. Adele Cantrell stood outside. Charli plastered a smile on her face and opened to Adele.

As before, the Frenchwoman's hair was perfectly styled, with loose auburn waves falling to her shoulders. With the expert application of her makeup and her stylish clothes, she could have stepped from the pages of a fashion magazine.

"Adele, please come in." Charli moved to let the other woman enter.

Adele swept into the house.

Charli shut the door. "Would you like some tea? Wine?"

Adele whirled around, her eyes cold. "This isn't a social visit."

Charli's smile faded, and chills skittered up her spine. "Oh? What kind of visit is it?"

"You Deveraux women are all the same." Malevolence colored Adele's voice.

Charli's stomach tightened and she pressed against the closed door. The hard wood dug into her back. "What do you mean by that?"

Adele stabbed a finger into Charli's chest. "You want what belongs to other women."

Adrenaline spiked through Charli. "Take your hand off me."

Stepping back, Adele stared at her with hate flashing in her eyes. "Louise wouldn't let Édouard go, even after she married Travis. She came after him, bewitching him, the way she bewitched all men. Now, my husband is taken with you because you look like her."

"Édouard has been very kind to Shannon and me. He's not indicated he wants anything more than friendship. I don't understand."

"I saw the way he looked at you during our dinner. He talks about you. He is attracted to you."

"There is nothing, and will never be anything, between your husband and me."

"See that is the case."

Hugging her purse, Adele sailed out.

Charli slammed the door shut and locked it, not quite sure what had just happened.

# CHAPTER TWENTY-SIX

W hen Shannon returned from the village, Charli told her about Adele's visit.

Shannon put groceries into a cabinet and closed the door. She met Charli's gaze. "That was crazy. Do you think she was threatening you?"

Charli shook her head. "Adele wasn't real friendly the evening they had us over, but she doesn't seem like the threatening type. I didn't feel scared from her visit, just surprised."

"Maybe she's insecure because her husband was in love with Louise and she's afraid it might happen again."

"That could be."

Shannon unscrewed the cap off a water bottle and sipped. "And maybe Adele is a murderer."

"She's no murderer."

"You're awfully quiet," Shannon said that night at dinner. "Still in a stew over Adele?"

"No, I'm okay with that. I'm thinking I'll have to get someone in here to break down that tower room door." Charli shivered. "Let's hope the tower opens to the turret room and there's not another missing key to get into that room."

"Bite your tongue. Don't even think that. We need to find the necklaces, or least what happened to them. And there might be some very valuable stuff in that room."

"Right."

"Once we're gone, you may never see Travis again. Are you okay with that?"

Charli pushed aside her empty plate and rested her elbows on the table. "I don't like to think about it. I've gotten to know him, and I like him. I'll miss him."

"Quit your job and stay here."

"My home is in Philadelphia. You know me. I don't like to make snap decisions. If I don't sell this property, I won't have any money to support myself here. If I sell it, I'll need another place here to live. Plus, I don't know if Travis would want me around."

"I think he'd very much like to keep you here." Shannon leaned closer. "You need to get out of your comfort zone. Have you learned nothing from me? I could have had a cushy corporate job out of art school but I took a chance on the graphic arts startup, and now look at me. I love my job." She put her hand over Charli's across the table. "I'm sorry. I don't mean to make you feel bad over your choice. You had to do what you thought best for you."

"You didn't have a boyfriend and a wedding to save for." Charli met Shannon's gaze. "That didn't turn out so well for me."

"Tim was a jerk and a coward. You should have taken one of his calls and called him every kind of name."

"I didn't want to talk to him."

"Water under the proverbial bridge now." Shannon released Charli's hand. "I need to go to London."

"That client?"

"Yes, he wants a face-to-face."

"You figured that might happen which is one of the reasons you came with me. Go. I know how important this is to you."

"I hate to leave you alone, with everything that happens around here."

"I'll be okay. You can't jeopardize your chance to secure this account. You have to go to London. Tomorrow Monsieur Belanger and the realtor are coming, and Travis is stopping by, too. He says he wants to make sure they don't try to cheat me."

"Travis would stay here with you while I'm gone if you asked. I'd feel better knowing you're not alone."

"I'll think about it." The anticipation of spending a few days alone with Travis set Charli's heart to racing.

# CHAPTER TWENTY-SEVEN

*T*he next day, Monsieur Belanger and the realtor had come and gone. Nursing cups of coffee, Travis and Charli sat in the kitchen.

Charli set down her cup and looked at Travis seated across from her. "The realtor pointed out some work this place could use to make it sell quicker. He made good points but I'm not sure it's necessary. Jeanne modernized this house and it doesn't need a lot of work."

"I agree."

"I appreciate your being here," she said.

He saluted. "Glad to be of assistance. Maybe some expat Brit will want to purchase it. All this land, the house, and the ruined tower."

She laughed. "What more could a person want?"

At her words, his eyes darkened. Something sparked between them. She shifted. What she wanted had nothing to do with houses, land, or towers.

Charli snatched her drink and sipped, watching him over the rim. Like the hot liquid burning her throat, her desire for Travis flamed higher every time he was near. It would have been safer for her heart had he continued to be gruff and rude, but he'd softened and shown himself to be a caring guy. That made him dangerous.

He broke their connection to walk to the counter to pour himself another coffee. He held the pot out to her. "More?"

"I'm good." *But I want to be bad with you.* Her face heated at her erotic thoughts. She hoped he didn't notice her blush.

Travis stared at her for long minutes, then sat back at the table and cradled his mug. "When do you think you'll have the place ready to put on the market?"

Charli relaxed, relieved to talk about something safe. "I thought I could come here, settle the estate, and put the house up, all in a month. I haven't finished going through it, and for sure I can't sell until I see what's in that turret room. Now that I know about the necklaces, I need to find them or find what happened to them." She sighed. "I may have to break down that beautiful door after all."

Travis reached across the table and took her hand. "Does this mean you'll be here longer?"

His touch incited a riot of longing in her. "Probably."

"I'd like you to stay longer."

"You would?"

He lifted her hand and brought it to his lips to plant a gentle kiss on her palm. He closed her fingers over her palm, sealing the kiss.

With reluctance, she pulled free. "I doubt I can take more time off work. My one-month leave is almost up."

"If you hate the job so much, why not resign now?"

"It pays the bills."

"You'll fetch a good price for Deveraux Manor."

"I don't know how long it will take to sell. I have a little money saved. I can use that to pay bills until this place is sold." She'd finally voiced what had been rolling around in her subconscious for days.

"You're a good artist. Maybe the time has come for you to take the leap of faith and devote yourself to art."

Charli ran a finger down the sides of her mug. "Art doesn't pay much, unless you're Jackson Pollock, Frank Stella, or someone like them."

"You draw and sketch to feed your soul."

"You could say that. My part-time work at my friend Chloe's gallery helps. I hope what I net from the sale of the estate will allow me to buy into the gallery."

He took more of his drink, then pushed away his mug, his attention still on her. "We both love art."

"We have something in common."

He scanned her face. His eyes settled on her mouth. "I think we've much more than art in common."

Charli glanced away, gathering her emotions around her like a blanket. Travis was coming to mean a lot to her. She didn't know if she was ready for another relationship. A small voice whispered to take a chance on him, to take a chance on life and living to the fullest. A kernel of fear blossomed in her. She'd always been so careful.

She needed to take her attention off her churning thoughts. Turning back to him, she asked, "How did you get into the art restoration business?"

He settled into his seat. "Almost by accident, but I love it and can't imagine doing anything else. I earned a degree in art history from university. I'm not as creative as I'm technical so art restoration works for me. My father wanted me to pursue business so I could take my place in the family company."

"I read your family owns one of the largest real estate development companies in Great Britain."

"My brother and a cousin help run the company now. I fought my father all through university, then when I graduated, I took a job as administrator of a small museum in London. My duties involved working with the art restorers. I watched them, fascinated, and knew that's what I wanted to do. One of the restorers took me under his wing and trained me."

"But your dad's not happy with your career choice."

Travis's features sobered. "My father figured I'd get art out of my system with the museum job and do what I *should* do, work for him. When he finally realized that wouldn't happen, we had a huge row, and I left London." A shadow passed over his face. "And here I am."

"Tell me a about your work. You restore paintings for museums and private collections?"

He nodded.

"As an art lover, I shouldn't find the story of the kids who threw their cereal bowls at a Picasso amusing. But I do. And I know you restored it to its original brilliance."

"I didn't tell you the whole story. The maid tried to clean it and almost destroyed it."

"Oh, no!"

He chuckled. "Oh, yes. My family has money but we don't have much art in our houses. We own a home in the Chelsea section of London and one they call a cottage, but it's more Downton Abbey, in the English countryside. Our homes are pretty traditional, what you'd expect from wealthy Brits, but I'm amazed at the way some of the super-rich live when I go to their houses for art restoration projects. I've been in mansions that look like dumps on the outside, but are filled with priceless art, and the other way around. I do a lot of work on yachts and private jets." He shook his head. "My family's company owns a jet, but my dad would rather live with the common folk in London than be so crass as to show an art collection on a plane."

Charli laughed. "Art on private jets?"

"The people who own the yachts and planes like to flaunt their wealth wherever they can."

Charli had never seen him so comfortable. She wanted to keep him talking about his work. "Tell me more."

"I once went to the home of a wealthy elderly gentleman. While I restored a painting by one of the masters, he and the very young maid were making loud love in the next room. I found it a tad distracting. I didn't care who the guy made love with, but he was a religious leader with a large family."

Charli almost choked on her coffee. "Hypocritical. But priceless."

Travis took her hand in his. His gaze held hers. "*You're* priceless, Charli. You make me feel alive for the first time in years."

She swallowed around the lump in her throat. Fear and excitement splashed through her like buckets of paint thrown on canvas.

CHAPTER TWENTY-EIGHT

*D*aylight faded to dusk as Travis told more tales about his jobs. Charli had never enjoyed herself so much, and with such a wildly attractive man.

"You must have some good stories to tell about the bank," he said.

"My job stories can't compete with yours about life among the rich and famous."

"This isn't a competition, Charli."

She glanced up at the ceiling, then back to him. "Here we go. Every full moon, Maisie the witch came into our downtown location."

"Maisie the witch? Sounds like a real character. Why did she come in during the full moon?"

"She said she had to protect the employees and the customers from the demons that would roam the streets when the moon rose."

"Maisie sounds like one of our British eccentrics. Did you throw her out of the bank?"

Charli finished her coffee and pushed the mug aside. "Two

cups of coffee are enough caffeine for me. My manager never threw her out. We all loved Maisie. She was harmless. The streets of Philadelphia are filled with characters, but not all are harmless."

Travis settled back in his seat. "Do you have more stories?"

"There was the time a woman ran into the bank screaming about witnessing a kidnapping. We called the police, who arrived in minutes."

"A kidnapping?"

She shook her head. "Not a real one. Students from a film class at a local high school were filming a movie about a kidnapping, but they never bothered to get permission from the city. Lots of embarrassment went around that day."

"I like your stories," he said.

"I love yours. This has been fun. I think it's time we made dinner. I'm hungry."

They shared additional laughs and companionship fixing a simple but delicious meal together— fresh mackerel Shannon had bought at the market the day before, a mixed green salad, and Pinot Grigio from the wine cellar.

Dinner over, they sat in the living room next to each other on one of the sofas, a sizzling fire in the marble fireplace, a comfortable silence between them. Charli sighed. "You live an interesting life, Travis. Much more compelling than my workaday world."

He skimmed a gentle finger down her face. "You, Charlotte Deveraux, are a very intriguing woman."

Longing for something deep and lasting pulled tight in her abdomen. "Thanks. I don't believe anyone has called me intriguing before."

"What is wrong with the men in Philadelphia?"

"I'm sure some are fine, but I haven't met many." She twisted to face him, tucking her legs under her. "Let's not talk about men in Philadelphia. Do you have any big jobs coming up?"

"Some restorations can take months. After Louise and I split,

I took whatever contracts would keep me away from France. I burned myself out. I came back to relax but I've had little of that."

He lifted his wine goblet from the coffee table in front of them and took a long sip. Holding the glass, he stared across the room. She waited for him, sensing he had more to say.

He turned back to her. She reached out a hand to smooth the pain and anguish from his eyes, but withdrew, knowing he wouldn't want her pity.

"The whole area has been roiled by Louise's murder. Deveraux doesn't have much crime, especially murders. There's a tension in the air that wasn't there before. This is a great little place, and I hate to see it marred like this."

"I watch a lot of police procedurals on TV. The perpetrator could be someone in Deveraux, someone known to many of the inhabitants." She shivered.

"Are you cold?" He drew her closer.

"No, just thinking Louise probably knew her killer." Charli rubbed her forehead. "I should tell you something."

"What is it?"

"Adele Cantrell came to see me the other day. Her visit was unusual."

He plunked his glass on the table. Wine sloshed over the sides and puddled on the tiled top. "What did she want?"

"Said her husband is attracted to me, that he never got over Louise, and I remind him of her." Charli swallowed. "I told her he's been friendly to me, and that's all."

Travis gathered her to him. "Adele is insecure where her husband is concerned. She didn't threaten you, did she?"

"I didn't get that from her."

"I'm glad I'm staying here with you while Shannon is away."

"So am I." Charli clung to him. His heartbeat against her cheek calmed her.

He pulled away and looked into her eyes. His green gaze,

dark and inviting, studied her. He bent toward her and kissed her. His lips, soft, yet firm, teased and cajoled. With a moan, she pressed closer and deepened the kiss, inviting his tongue to take possession of her. Their tongues sparred and mated. Flaming heat engulfed her.

She leaned back on the sofa, and he followed. His taut body covered hers. He left her mouth to press his lips to her collarbone. Tiny cries she barely recognized as her own escaped her.

The doorbell rang, sudden and persistent, throwing ice water on her libido. She pushed away and sat up, putting distance between herself and the too-appealing man who made her forget her inhibitions. Having him so close could wreck her self-control. For many reasons, she couldn't allow herself to fall for him. Her heart didn't agree.

The doorbell rang again, more insistent.

"It's almost nine. Kind of late for someone to be coming here," she said.

Travis released a breath and stood. "That must be Max with my things. I called him after you asked me to stay." He raked fingers through his hair and looked down at his groin. "His timing sucks. I need to wait a while before I answer."

The bell rang again.

Charli stood on shaky legs and ran her hands down the sides of her jeans. "I'll get the door."

<><><>

Max brought over clothes and essentials for Travis, and Charli showed Travis to his room. Despite the hot kiss they'd shared, she wouldn't meet his eyes. He wanted to reach for her, gather her to him, but he sensed she needed space.

He settled into one of the smaller bedrooms on the second floor, furnished sparsely with a double bed, nightstand and dresser. The room shared a bath with a second small bedroom.

He spent a restless night colored with erotic dreams of going to Charli's room and making passionate love to her. Having her sleeping doors away was torture.

The next morning, he went into the kitchen to find Charli at the table, coffee mug and a plate of croissants from the village patisserie in front of her. He went to her and touched her chin with his fingers until she lifted her gaze to his. Her soft full lips parted, tempting him to feast on them. He bent and kissed her gently, then took a seat opposite her.

Her face turned a pretty shade of pink. She might be a little conflicted about their growing relationship, but she wasn't immune to him. Today promised to be a good one because he'd spend it with her.

The night before, they'd agreed to go over everything they knew about Louise's life and murder. Papers were spread over the table.

"'Morning. Did you sleep well?" The slight tremble in Charli's voice provoked a smile from him.

"Very," he lied. Her wholesome beauty made his heart lurch. Her thick, long dark hair fell over her shoulders, and kindness shone from her large blue-gray eyes. He wanted to grab her to him and bury his face in her luxurious hair, to find comfort and hope in her arms. Fear intruded. If he got too close to her, she might take his heart with her when she left.

She gestured to the carafe and mugs on the table. "Have some coffee and a croissant."

He poured himself coffee and slipped a delicate pastry onto a plate. "What have you got there?"

She waved her hand over the sheets of paper. "Information I collected. So far, I have no suspect, unless Édouard killed Louise. Maybe he got into a jealous rage because she took other lovers."

Travis surveyed the table, then met her gaze. "I'm the one who flew into a jealous rage."

Charli widened her eyes. "What?"

He scrubbed a hand down his face. "I can understand why the police targeted me as her killer at first. Louise and I were at an outdoor café in the village when she confessed she wasn't pregnant. She also threw it into my face that she took lovers. Her words sent me over the edge. We had a screaming fight, right there, in full view of the villagers. I'm not proud of that."

Charli put her hand over his across the table. "Oh, Travis, how terrible, for both you and Louise."

"If my mother could have seen me, she'd have a coronary. According to her, we Gardners don't act like the working class."

"You had reasons."

"Yes, but I'm ashamed of myself for losing my temper like that. It's not something I've done often."

"The only serious boyfriend I ever had cheated on me. I was devastated. I can't imagine how it was with you."

"How long ago did this happen, with your boyfriend marrying someone else?"

Charli grabbed a croissant and bit into it, chewing slowly, as if she hadn't heard him. Finally, she said, "Two years, but I'm pretty much over it." She looked adorably sweet, and he fought not to take her into his arms.

"Are you?"

She cleared her throat. "Since Louise had more than one lover, that makes our job a little harder." Charli wasn't ready to talk about her ex. Travis would give her the time she needed.

He picked up his coffee, drinking before setting the mug down. "It may not have been one of her lovers who killed her."

"True. Édouard told us Adele has a lover. Taking lovers isn't the sort of marriage I want."

"What do you want, Charli?"

She gripped her mug, not looking at him. "I want an equal partnership in a marriage. I want a man who will be loyal to me, as I will be to him."

"It's what I always wanted, too," he said quietly.

"I don't want to judge Louise, but the whole thing is sordid. Makes me glad my grandparents left here for America."

"It's not the place where you are brought up. It's the people around you who determine the kind of person you'll be. You had good people who raised you."

"Louise didn't?"

"Jeanne did her best, but Louise was a handful, and Jeanne didn't like to be strict, so Louise was allowed to run around without boundaries, even as a child."

"That's too bad. I was always a good child who did what she was told. My parents never had a problem with me."

He stared at her, assessing her words. "Have you never taken a chance on something you wanted to do?"

"Not really. Shannon had to talk me into coming here." Charli blushed and turned back to the papers. "Let's continue here."

"Okay. Any thoughts?"

"Did Louise have friends nearby? People who might know who she fooled around with?"

He frowned. "Most of her friends live in Paris. Fontaine, the detective, interviewed her friends there and in Rouen. They all acknowledged Louise had several lovers. They gave Fontaine the names of the ones they knew of. He questioned every man and found each had an ironclad alibi. None of her friends mentioned Baptiste Riviere, but I caught them together once."

"The plumber? No wonder you don't like him. Did your detective question him?"

"He did, and Baptiste had an alibi. He was on a job in the next town."

Charli pursed her lips. "Another dead end. There must be someone who stayed in the shadows, someone who had a lot to lose if it came out he and Louise were lovers."

"Or someone she'd just met and whom she took home with her. Although Louise made my life hell, I didn't wish her dead."

"I believe you."

The warmth in her eyes provoked him to want to gather her to him and kiss her sweet lips. Travis stayed seated. He didn't want to frighten her away from him.

# CHAPTER TWENTY-NINE

The day passed quickly. They found no clues to bring them closer to discovering Louise's killer, but Charli had enjoyed brainstorming possible scenarios with Travis. They searched again for the tower key but came up empty.

Despite her frustrations, she'd enjoyed her day with him. He was good company, easy to talk to, easy on the eyes, too. After dinner, needing to clear their heads, they walked to the ruined tower.

Travis took her hand as they strolled. Charli didn't pull away. The full moon lit a silvery path for them. Night birds sang and insects chirped. Charli inhaled the flower-scented air. Peace, mixed with excitement, stole over her.

When they got to the tower, Travis wound his arm around her waist and pulled her to him. She pillowed her head against his shoulder. She never wanted the moment to end.

"It's so tranquil here." She stared at the sky. "There are more stars than I've ever seen."

"We're in the country. Not as many artificial lights from Earth to interfere with the heavens."

He gripped her shoulders and pushed her gently away. His eyes, hot and wicked, stirred something deep and yearning within her. She reached up a hand and touched the pads of her fingers to his soft, full lips.

"Charli." His eyes drifted to her mouth, and he caressed her cheek with his thumb, then ran his hands over her shoulders and down her arms. Pulling her to him, he took her lips in a desperate kiss, urgent and hungry.

He buried his hands in her hair, provoking a soft moan from her. She breathed in his scent of the outdoors and kissed him like a woman starved, devouring his lips, delighting in the taste and feel of him.

She opened her mouth to his invasion. Their tongues mated. Her nipples swelled and tightened, aching for him. He moved his hands to her waist and pulled her tighter to him. His erection pressed against her stomach. He left her mouth to trail kisses down her chin to her neck and behind her ear. She threw her head back, giving herself to him.

His spicy scent mingled with the outdoors galvanized her pulse. Her whole body tingled. One of his big hands slid under her shirt and cupped her breast. The heated area between her thighs burned for him. She uttered small cries she barely recognized as her own.

Her heart rate sped up. She wanted him to make love to her right there, outdoors. She'd never made love outdoors before. "Travis," she moaned into his mouth.

He ended the kiss abruptly, but held her against his chest. The loud thumping of his heart matched hers. The air chilled her.

*No*, she wanted to scream. She looked up at him. "What's wrong?"

"I won't take advantage of you, Charli," he said.

"You're not."

With a smile, he brushed her lips in a whisper-soft kiss, then took her hand in his.

They walked back to the manor hand-in-hand.

Conflicting emotions clogged Charli's throat. She craved his touch, his kisses, wanted him as she'd never wanted another man. She'd been ready to make love to him there, by the tower. She should be grateful he'd stopped. Why did she feel so…cheated?

When they reached the house, Travis did another security check before they headed to their rooms. They stopped at Charli's bedroom. She put a hand on the doorknob and turned to him. "Good night. Maybe we'll have better luck tomorrow." She smiled. "I loved spending the day with you."

The surprise that flitted across his face matched her own. The words had come from somewhere deep inside her and she'd blurted them.

"It's my pleasure to spend time with you, Charli."

"Travis." She breathed his name. "Come to bed with me." She'd never asked a man to make love to her. They'd grown close, and she could no longer deny what she so desperately needed.

"You're sure?"

She stood on tiptoe and brushed a tender kiss on his full, inviting lips. "Surer than I've ever been about anything in my life. I was willing back at the tower. I need you." She looked down then back up to him. "Unless you don't feel the same."

"I just showed you how I felt at the tower."

"Why did you stop?"

"I told you. I can't take advantage of you."

"Take advantage. I give you permission."

With a loving grin, he kissed her, his lips firm and demanding. She turned the doorknob, and they fell into the room together, still locked in their kiss. Travis backed her up against the wall. Heat seeped into her belly and lower.

His lips teased hers open. He eased his tongue between her teeth. A twisting, needy fire built inside her. He left her mouth to rain hot kisses down her throat. His long fingers traced her ribcage and hips.

When he slipped a hand under her shirt, Charli's body felt weightless. Moaning softly, she wrapped her arms around his waist. He massaged her breast with his hand, and bent to take one pebbled nipple into his mouth, through the thin fabric of her shirt.

On fire, she knew only Travis, wanted only him. Damn the past and damn the future. All that mattered was him, his heat, his passion, the wildness he incited in her.

His lips on hers, he lifted her and carried her to the bed. Holding her, he pulled back the comforter and sheet. Ending the kiss, he laid her on the bed as if she was a delicate work of art. With exquisite tenderness, he undressed her until she lay naked in front of him.

He closed his eyes for seconds, his breathing shallow. When he met her gaze again, his eyes sparked green fire.

"You are more beautiful than I imagined," he rasped.

"Take off your clothes. I want to see all of you." She didn't know where her new boldness came from, but she liked it. Her need for Travis dissolved her hang-ups.

He shed his clothes, exposing his beauty to her. The mattress squeaked in protest as he lowered himself next to her. She leaned over him. Her hair grazed the smattering of dark hairs on his chest, and she ran her fingers over his firm abs.

He slipped his hand beneath her hair and cradled the back of her head. She took his lips in a ravenous kiss. Her breasts rubbed his chest, eliciting groans from him.

Travis gripped her buttocks, pressing her against his hard erection. Filled with feminine power, she moved slowly over him, teasing.

Finally, he wrapped her hair around his hand and gently pulled her away. "I won't last if you keep doing that."

"I want you so much."

"We have all night."

"I need you now."

His smile ignited the burning ache between her legs. He slid out from her and reached over to pick up his jeans from the floor. Digging into a pocket, he pulled out a foil packet.

Charli took it from him and opened it. Slowly and carefully, she drew the protection onto his throbbing cock.

Sexual urgency tightened his face. He held her upper arms and rolled her under him. She opened her arms in invitation.

He positioned his body over hers. Aching for him to fill her, she parted her legs for him. He entered her easily. His scent of aroused male filled her soul as his hardness filled her body. She surrendered to him, to the essence that was Travis. He moved his hips slowly over hers, and suckled one breast, then the other, telling her without words how beautiful he found her.

He drove into her heat. She tunneled her hands through the thickness of his hair and met his every thrust. Liquid fire raced through her veins. Like a drug, he possessed her, made her crave him with every part of her. She reveled at his groans of longing.

His touch seared her flesh, and desire rushed at a fevered pace through her. Nothing but the sheen of sweat separated them. He pounded harder, taking her higher and higher. She spiraled out of control.

Her orgasm built in smoldering waves, consuming her. She cried out his name and clutched his back, lost in him, lost in passion she'd never known.

He stilled, then shouted his own climax.

They held each other until their breathing settled. Finally, he slid off her and pulled the covers over them. He gathered her to him.

Settled in the crook of his arm, Charli felt satiated, whole. She'd come home.

Travis kissed her temple. "Are you all right?"

Cuddling against him, she kissed his throat and the light

stubble on his jaw. "Better than ever." She chewed her lip. Truth be told, she'd only had two lovers, both tepid. Neither had brought her to the heights like Travis.

He pulled her tighter against him. "You inspire me."

# CHAPTER THIRTY

Charli stretched like a contented cat. Languid and sated, she wanted to purr. Sunlight teased her eyes open. Sun! A good omen.

She swept her tongue over her lips, swollen and sensitive from Travis's kisses. Last night, he opened her to a world of sensual delights. They'd made love into the wee hours. Orgasm after orgasm had shattered her, fulfilling her every sensual fantasy. Charli smiled at the memory. She could make love with him all day. He'd released the wild woman inside her. Freed, that woman would never again hide.

Travis had lifted the veil over her emotions. Tim had been a comfortable habit, and after seeing the devastation her dad suffered after he lost her mom, Charli kept her feelings tight around her. She'd missed so much, but she determined to make up for lost time.

With a satisfied moan, she reached out to touch the place next to her on the bed. Her hand met cool sheet, but no Travis. Rubbing sleep from her eyes, she sat up, clutching the comforter to her chest.

"Travis!" Silence greeted her.

Insecurity reared up, clouding her high spirits. Had their lovemaking meant nothing to Travis and he'd walked out on her?

A soft knock on the bedroom door, followed by the door opening, pulled her attention from her sobering thoughts. Travis, dressed in tight-fitting jeans that molded to his muscular frame, stood in the doorway holding a tray. Despite her anxiety, Charli feasted her eyes on his bare chest, his firm abs, his defined muscles.

"I brought breakfast." He advanced toward the small table flanked by chairs and set down the tray. Platters of scrambled eggs, toast, tomatoes, along with a carafe and two mugs rested on the tray. "Let's eat, and afterwards, we'll take a ride to Rouen. The weather is perfect."

"That sounds great, but I have a lot to do here."

A sexy grin on his face, he stalked to the bed and sat next to her. He pulled her close. Her sheet drifted down, exposing her naked breasts. His eyes darkened.

He touched the tip of her nose with his finger. "We deserve a day of fun."

She gave him what she hoped was a saucy smile. "We had lots of fun last night. We could stay here in bed all day and have more fun."

"You are a naughty woman. I would like nothing better than making love with you from now to dark, but I want to spend time with you, outside of bed, and get to know Charlotte Deveraux." He planted a ravenous kiss on her waiting lips, then trailed kisses down her throat to her chest. Her nipples puckered and her breasts felt heavy. He massaged her breasts, eliciting moans from her.

"I'm hungry for you," she whispered.

His passion-glazed eyes met hers. "Breakfast can wait."

<><><>

Charli and Travis drove in his Mercedes, heading for Rouen. Although the sun rode high in the sky among soft clouds, the day was chilly. She'd worn jeans, a sweater, ankle boots, and a light jacket. Back home, they were having a heat wave with highs in the 90's. She missed the warmth, but Travis wasn't in Philly. She'd rather be here with him. The thought jolted her.

She slid a glance at his strong profile as he drove. He was beautiful, with high cheekbones and a hawk-like nose. His black hair hugged the curve of his neck. Her hands and lips had been all over him last night and this morning. She craved the touch of his firm body, his silky hair, his full lips.

She loved his kindness to her and Shannon. The affection he felt for Max was obvious in the respect he showed his old friend. Travis Gardner had facets she yearned to discover. She'd leave before she had a chance to know all of him. Regret punched her in the stomach.

*You've got it bad, girl.* So long as she didn't fall in love with Travis, she'd enjoy him while she was here. Years from now, he'd be a pleasant memory of the man who'd awakened her sexual desire, but her heart would be intact.

A little voice whispered, *too late.*

"On the way here, we took a train from Paris to Rouen," Charli said in an attempt to shut down her uncomfortable thoughts. "It was raining and we were jet-lagged. We had no time to look around."

Travis glanced her way. "You'll love Rouen. It's a charming Medieval town. I don't know if you're religious, but Joan of Arc was burned at the stake there."

"I learned about her in school. Can we see where it happened?"

"We'll be tourists today, visiting all the sites, walking the cobblestoned streets. I'll take you to my favorite café for dinner. Small Rouen contains several Michelin-starred restaurants." Pride colored his voice.

"You love it here."

He reached over the console and grabbed her hand where it lay on the leather seat. "I fell in love with Normandy the first time I visited. I think you'll learn to love it too."

"I already do." The beauty of the lush rolling hills spoke to her soul. Perhaps it was in her DNA. Or maybe it was the man next to her.

They found a parking spot on a narrow street off the market square. Travis held her elbow as they strode along the ancient cobblestones. Like a child on Christmas morning, Charli gazed in wonder at the colorful timber houses dating from the Middle Ages that lined the perimeter of the square.

She stopped suddenly at the sight before her. "Look at that clock." A stunning enormous clock, gilt and blue, hung above an arch at the end of the square.

"That's something, isn't it? The Gros-Horlog is a fourteenth century astronomical clock. You may have seen it in some famous paintings."

"Magnificent."

People strode around them, some in a hurry, others meandering. A group of tourists stood in front of the arch staring up at the clock. The flag their tour guide held announced the group was from one of the ships that routinely traveled the Seine. The river wove through Rouen, dividing it into two banks.

"I want to experience it all," Charli said. "But first, Joan of Arc."

Travis took her hand in his and smiled down at her. "There's a lot to see in one day, but we'll be back many times, I hope."

Charli wished that too, but reality snuck in. She pushed it aside. Only today mattered.

Holding hands, they strolled to the site where Joan of Arc met her death. Charli bent her head and sent a silent prayer for strength to the brave saint who'd fought and died for her beliefs. Charli, afraid to quit a job she hated, drew inspiration from the brave St. Joan who sacrificed her life to help her country.

Later, Charli and Travis sat in pews enjoying the quiet of Rouen's Notre Dame Cathedral. In awe over the majesty of the architecture, surprising hope rushed through Charli that she and Travis could have a future together, even though his life was in Normandy, and hers was in Philadelphia. For the first time, she began to believe they could make a relationship work.

They bought fresh produce and baked goods at the Clos Saint-Marc market. Travis put the food in the trunk of his car, then, taking Charli's hand, he led her to a tiny restaurant tucked into a corner of a side street.

A man wearing a suit smiled when they entered and hurried over to them. He spoke French to Travis and nodded to Charli, then showed them to a small round table in an alcove next to the fireplace, where a low fire burned to take the chill off the late June day.

"What a quaint place," Charli said when she sat at the table. "They seem to know you here."

"I come here often. The owner, Monsieur Arquette, has been a friend since I first came to Normandy."

Travis ordered a bottle of Bordeaux and translated the menu for Charli. She wanted to order Rouen's famed dish, the Rouen duckling, until she learned one of the ingredients was thickened blood. She settled on Poulet Vallée d'Auge, a traditional Norman dish of crème fraiche, chicken, heavy cream, Calvados, apple cider, onions, and mushrooms. While they sipped the rich wine, Travis said, "Tell me more about Charlotte Deveraux."

"Ask away."

"What is your favorite color?"

"Yellow."

"Favorite movie."

She laughed and took a sip of wine before answering. "Would you believe *The Terminator*?"

He threw back his head and laughed. "Really? Why?"

"It's a good story. It's hopeful and has a romance."

"Favorite TV show."

"*Criminal Minds.*"

"I've seen it. It's a violent show." A grin played around the corners of his mouth. "Are you trying to tell me something, Charlotte?"

"Despite those shows, I really hate violence."

"What's your favorite book? Something by Stephen King?"

With a laugh, she pushed aside her empty wine glass. The waiter ran over and refilled it. "Asking me to choose a favorite book is like asking a mother to choose which child she prefers. I read a lot. My Kindle has over 1500 books." She tapped her finger to her chin. "If I had to pick one, I'd say *Green Darkness* by Anya Seton."

"Why that one?"

"It has a love story that spans time, lots of history, reincarnation, some violence. I'm fascinated by the concept of reincarnation."

"You're open to magic, the occult, witchcraft?"

The cat on her bed shot into her mind. It had seemed so real, not a dream at all. She couldn't tell him about the cat. Travis would think her bonkers. "Some of it is too fantastical to be real."

"Do you believe in ghosts?"

Charli took a sip of the fortifying wine. "I don't. It's hard to wrap my mind around the concept of spirits."

"There are people who swear they've seen the ghosts of Andre and Dominique Deveraux." He smiled. "Even a white ghost cat with them."

"A ghost cat?" She swallowed. "I think I saw the cat." There, it was out. She stared at him, waiting for him to tell her she was nuts.

He watched her without speaking. "Do you think I'm crazy?" she blurted.

"Of course not." He took her hand across the table. "I believe there are forces around us that aren't of this world."

# CHAPTER THIRTY-ONE

"*T*hat was amazing." Charli slid off Travis's chest and flopped onto the mattress.

He leaned over her. Her beautiful face was flushed from their lovemaking, and her plump lips were red. When they returned from Rouen last evening, they'd ripped their clothes off as they headed to the bedroom. They'd made love again at dawn, and now as the sun rose in the sky.

He brushed strands of her hair off her face and looked deeply into her large, expressive eyes, shining now with happiness. "*You* are amazing."

Charli lifted herself up and touched her lips to his, then lay back on her pillow. "What have you done to me? I didn't know lovemaking could be like this, consuming me. I want to make love to you all the time."

Travis laughed. "I'll be glad to oblige. You're a passionate woman, Charli." He took her in his arms, holding her tight.

"No one has ever said that to me before."

"No one took the time to see the real you."

She wiggled against him, eliciting a groan from him.

"You keep doing that and I'll have to take you again," he growled. "Over and over."

She raised up on her elbow and looked down at him with passion-filled eyes. "Promise?"

Much later they sat in the kitchen finishing the mushroom omelet Travis had cooked. Charli slid her last piece of egg into her mouth and wrapped her lips around the fork. He could not look away. He was hungry for her again, but they had to leave soon to meet Shannon, arriving from London today, at the Rouen train station. He'd sleep in his own bed tonight. Alone.

Pangs of regret twisted in his stomach. He'd miss Charli's warmth, her laughter, her joy, making love to her all night. He reached across the table and took her hand in his.

Her soft, warm eyes met his. He rubbed his fingers over the back of her hand. "Yesterday with you was one of the best days of my life. Your excitement made me see Rouen and everything around it in a new light."

"It was a day I'll always remember."

He released her hand. "Why does that sound so final?"

"Travis, what's between us is special. You've awakened something in me, taught me a little about myself. Every minute with you has been a beautiful dream." Unshed tears made her eyes sparkle like diamonds. "Once this house is cleaned of everything valuable, I'll put it on the market. My home is in Philadelphia."

"You could stay here."

She stood. "I need to take a shower and get dressed."

Disappointment held him in his seat. He'd scared her. He wanted to laugh at himself. Had he really expected her to declare her undying love? He was a fool.

He stood too. "I'll join you in the shower."

<><><>

Dominique, perched on the kitchen counter, swung her legs

and turned to Andre, leaning against the counter opposite her. "I am distressed at Charli's attitude. Travis was giving her his heart and she refused it."

"Give her time," Andre said. "She is confused and scared by her feelings for Travis."

"They are healing, but they must fall in love and acknowledge that love."

Andre put his arm around her shoulders and drew her close. "Have faith. We will succeed in our mission and everyone will be happy."

<><><>

Travis left for his place after dropping Shannon and Charli at Deveraux Manor, but not before he planted a passionate kiss on Charli's lips.

As he drove away, Shannon folded her arms across her chest and tapped her foot, a grin splitting her face. "Want to tell me what that was about?"

Charli pretended to flick lint off her jacket. "What was what about?"

"Don't play innocent. That kiss. What the heck went on here while I was away?"

"Let's talk over tea."

Seated in the kitchen, with cups of steaming mint tea and a plate of cream puffs Travis and Charli had bought in Rouen, the women stared at each other. Charli knew tenacious Shannon wouldn't leave the room until she got every detail of the past days.

"Travis and I made love." Charli's face burned. "Lots of times."

"High five, girlfriend." Shannon held up her hand and leaned closer.

Grinning, Charli slapped her palm with Shannon's. "I guess it is pretty incredible." She looked down at the table, remembering all she and Travis had done. "Travis is incredible." She met Shannon's gaze again. "Of course, I can only compare him with two other men, and trust me, there's no comparison."

"About time you made love with a *real* man."

Charli plucked a pastry from the plate and bit into it, relishing its deliciousness.

"I think you love him." Shannon's lips tilted in a wry smile. "Not that I know much about love. After that disastrous engagement with *he who shall not be named*." She placed her hand over Charli's across the table. "Don't be afraid. Listen to your heart. Trust your instincts. Trust Travis."

Charli grabbed her tea to wash down the pastry that had gotten stuck in her throat at Shannon's words.

Coughing, she found her voice. "In love? What makes you say that?"

"The dreamy look on your face. He's a decent guy. He's been good to us, good to you."

"I'm not sure yet how I feel about him." Charli ran her fingers over the smooth surface of the table. "I like him a lot, and I like being with him." She raised her eyes to Shannon. "Things are happening too fast. Change and spontaneous decisions make my chest tighten. I'm afraid I'll be hurt again."

"And it's easier for you to focus on his lovemaking than admit you might be in love with him."

"You know me too well."

"I love you and I want you to get the happiness you deserve."

Charli sighed and looked down at the table. "Thanks. Tim and I never had a lot of passion to begin with. I'm not so bitter anymore because of what he did to me. Now that I've been with Travis, I understand why Tim fell in love so fast with that other woman. Maybe he was looking for passion too, for that person that made his heart sing."

She met Shannon's gaze. "Travis makes my heart sing."

"I know he does. Maybe Tim wanted to apologize when he called you all those times after the breakup. You need closure with him."

"Maybe I'll call him."

"Good idea. Get that closure, then concentrate on your relationship with Travis."

"Let's talk about you. How was London?"

"We got the contract."

"Congrats. What was your client like?"

A faraway look came into Shannon's hazel eyes. "Niall was very nice and friendly. Gracious. Very British. He took me to lunch and dinner and even a play."

"Niall, huh? How old is this guy?"

Shannon's eyes sparkled. "About my age. Single. Good-looking."

"I think someone is infatuated."

"He's a client. Nothing more."

"Yeah, right. You deserve a good man after what happened to you with *he who shall not be named.*"

"Let's forget men for a while."

Charli looked away, though Travis was always on her mind. Soon they'd be separated by an ocean. Hope mingled with the waves of sadness that washed over her. Maybe she and Travis could find a way to be together.

Charli pushed up from her seat. "I'll be back. I'm going to get my closure now before I lose my nerve."

She headed to her room, pulling her cell phone from her pocket as she walked. In her room, she leaned against the door, took deep breaths, and punched in the familiar number. It was early afternoon back in Philly.

Tim answered on the second ring. "Charli? Is it really you?"

"Hello, Tim. Yes, it's me calling from France."

"I heard about your inheritance. I'm happy for you."

An awkward silence followed. Finally, Charli said, "How's Emily?"

"She's good. We're expecting a baby."

In the past, Tim's words would have filled Charli with despair. She'd always thought she and Tim would have a child together. Now, she felt only gladness for him.

"That's good, Tim."

"Charli, I'm really sorry for what I did. I was a coward. I should have come to you and explained everything. What I did to you was inexcusable."

"Yes, it was. You hurt me badly, and I didn't deserve that."

"Can you forgive me?"

"I think I can. I've met someone, here in France. It may take a while for me to totally forgive you, but I wanted you to know I'm fine, and I understand now why you fell so hard for Emily. My feelings for Travis have opened my heart."

"Thank you, Charli. That means a lot to me. Good luck with your new guy."

"Goodbye, Tim." She disconnected the call and threw the phone onto the bed. Tears gathered in her eyes. She had closure. With that call, her old life peeled away for good. She hoped she had the courage to finally take a chance on a new life.

CHAPTER THIRTY-TWO

The next morning, breakfasted and freshly showered, Charli dressed in her room. Her bed had been lonely last night without Travis. Although, they'd slept together only two nights, she'd felt comfortable with him, as if they'd been lovers for years. Lovers with an insatiable need for each other.

She pulled on her jeans, then a sweater. Opening a dresser drawer, she reached for her belt before remembering Shannon had brought it with her to London. Charli left her bedroom and strode to the stairs leading to the third floor. She called up to Shannon working in the small office.

No response. Charli took the stairs two at a time and opened the study door to peek inside. Shannon typed on her laptop, her phone on the desk. She wore earbuds and tapped her foot, no doubt to music playing on the phone. Charli grinned. Shannon liked headbanger music, the louder, the better. No wonder she hadn't heard her calling. Not wanting to disturb her friend, Charli closed the door and trod down to Shannon's room. She found her belt lying on the dresser.

Threading the belt through the loops on her jeans, Charli went into her room.

And screamed.

A woman, legs crossed, sat on the dresser. Although she trembled all over, Charli's feet were stuck. She couldn't move.

"Bonjour, Charli. My name is Dominique Deveraux. No need to fear me. I am here to help." She spoke English with a strong French accent.

Her vocal chords frozen, her breathing rapid, and her heart pumping hard, Charli stared at the woman. Beautiful, with her blonde hair in a short bob, she wore a flowing print dress that looked like silk, the style from the 1930's. The dress was torn in places and spotted with something she guessed was blood.

"Dominique," Charli squeaked out. She sidled to the wall and leaned against it, not trusting her legs to hold her. "The woman in the newspaper clipping. You died. In 1933. You're wearing the dress in the picture."

"Yes, I am the woman who died too young. Sadly, we spirits are stuck with the clothes we, uh…left the world in." She chuckled. "Poor Marie Antoinette, forced to endure that ugly gown for eternity. And old Ben Franklin with those silly knickers and stockings."

"This can't be real. I'm dreaming." Charli had to be in the middle of a very life-like dream.

The woman rubbed her fingernails along the shoulder of her dress, then studied the nails before gazing back at Charli. "I am here. You are not dreaming."

Charli edged along the bedroom wall, putting distance between herself and the specter sitting on her dresser. *There are no such things as ghosts* she repeated like a mantra. *I am not going crazy.*

Dominique chuckled. "Yes, there is such a thing as ghosts and you are not crazy."

"You can read minds."

"I can read your thoughts on your face. Your face is very

expressive, and very pretty. You resemble Louise, but with an inner beauty Louise never possessed."

"You knew Louise?" Charli put a hand to her chest to calm her racing heart.

Sadness flashed across the ghost's face. "She was a Deveraux, a descendant of my dear husband Andre. We were supposed to help her, but we failed."

"Failed?"

"That is not important."

Charli looked around. "Is Andre here?" Just what she needed, not one, but two ghosts.

"He is not here. We thought it better if only I appear to you. And Angel." Dominique nodded toward the bed. "Mon Ange, come to me."

Charli tightened her shoulders and blinked rapidly, turning slowly to the bed. She screamed again. Damn Shannon and those earbuds. And her headbanger music.

A long-haired white cat reclined on the comforter, staring at Charli with yellow eyes. The cat stood and stretched its long body, then leapt into Dominique's arms.

Charli whimpered. "I saw that cat before." Her voice shook.

Dominique petted the cat which was now lying on her lap. "Mon Ange was a bad girl, showing herself to you like that. She likes to tease, isn't that right, Angel?"

"Her name is Angel?" With effort, Charli relaxed her muscles. Demons wouldn't name a cat Angel, would they? Dominique wasn't evil. She hoped. Charli sank down into the nearest chair and gripped the arms until her knuckles whitened.

"What do you want, Dominique? And why haven't you and Andre, and Angel, even Marie Antoinette and Franklin gone to the light? How many spirits are there around here?" She was babbling. She scanned the room, wondering if more ghosts would jump out at her.

"There are spirits around all the time. Some of us, like Andre and I, choose not to leave the mortal world for fear of what lies beyond. Andre and I haunted Deveraux Village and the manor for decades. Finally, bored, we decided to go to the light."

Dominique looked away, then met Charli's gaze. The spirit's blue eyes sparkled with tears. "We followed the light but it didn't lead to Heaven."

"Where did it lead?"

"A dreary, cold place we call the holding place. Some call it Purgatory."

"I know about Purgatory. Don't you go to Heaven after a certain period of time?" Charli put a hand to her mouth. She was carrying on a conversation with a ghost. She was losing her mind, or in a dream to end all dreams.

"If we redeem ourselves, we can go to a better place. We all get the chance at redemption, but many fail. Andre and I were not evil in life, but we were selfish. When God's Angel came to us a year ago with an offer to redeem ourselves, we took it. Alas, our selfishness prevailed and we failed. We were sent back. We made another deal with the Big Guy. We cannot fail this time. I will not go back to that place."

Charli gulped breaths. "The Big Guy?"

Dominique pointed to the ceiling, then jumped down from the dresser, still holding Angel. "Andre and I want to help you and Travis find your destiny and also discover who killed Louise. Had we done what we'd been tasked with the first time, Louise would still be alive."

"What?"

"Never mind. Perhaps things have worked the way they were intended. Had Louise not died, you and Travis wouldn't have met." Dominique's eyes widened. "God's ways are mysterious, non?"

"If you say so. You and Andre are going to help us find the killer? And our destiny?" Charli needed to wake up soon. Wait until she told Shannon about her crazy dream.

Dominique's pretty face tightened. "You cannot leave France until you have fulfilled your purpose and brought Louise's killer to justice."

Charli licked her lips and swallowed. "Is Louise a ghost, too?"

Dominique floated over to the bed and sat, releasing Angel. The mattress never dipped with her weight.

"Don't fret. Louise is in a place where she can't escape." Dominique crossed herself. "At least we hope that is the case."

"You hope!" Charli clenched her hands on the chair arms, fighting a new burst of fear.

"Andre and I will protect you."

"Tell me where to search for the tower key." Charli might as well pretend she believed a ghost was sitting feet away.

"Jeanne kept it on her. We were not here when she died. We suspect Louise took it. She spent much time in the wine cellar. Maybe if you and your friend search, you'll find something."

Dominique touched the corner of her mouth with a manicured finger. Her lips glistened with ruby red lipstick. "I cannot appear to you too many times, but there is one other thing we need you to do."

"Why can't you appear to me?" Did she really want a ghost to keep showing herself?

"Each time we appear to a mortal, we lose a little of our essence."

"What happens then?"

"If we lose all our essence, we spend eternity in Purgatory."

"Oh. I hope that doesn't happen. What do you need me to do?"

"We suspect our car accident was not an accident. We believe Andre's brother Maurice cut the brakes. Maurice thought he should inherit more from their father as he was the son who stayed home and helped. Maurice's gambling debts made him desperate."

Sadness flashed over Dominique's face and she shook her

head. "Andre and I partied too much. Andre couldn't be bothered with the estate. Maurice was in a rage when the contents of the will were revealed and Andre got the bulk of the fortune. Please try to find proof Maurice killed us. You must get justice for Andre and me also." She stood and swept a hand down her dress. "Time for me to go."

Charli stood, too, on legs that were steady now. "Please tell me, where are the necklaces?"

"I cannot say." With that, Dominique faded, Angel with her.

Blinking, Charli stared at where Dominique had been.

"Charli?" Shannon called from the hall.

The bedroom door opened and Shannon peeked in. "Who were you talking to? My God, what's wrong? You're as white as a ghost."

"Ghosts wear colorful silk dresses."

## CHAPTER THIRTY-THREE

S hannon took Charli's hand and led her down the stairs to the kitchen. She sat Charli at the table while she boiled water for tea. When the tea was ready, Shannon pressed a mug into her hands. "Drink up. You need it."

Charli inhaled the scent of chamomile, then took a long swallow, enjoying the slide of the calming brew down her throat. Cradling the mug, she met Shannon's concerned gaze. "I need wine."

"Later. Want to tell me what happened? What was that about ghosts wearing colorful silk?"

With her hands still wrapped around the mug, Charli lowered her head, taking measured breaths before meeting Shannon's eyes again. "I met Dominique Deveraux."

Shannon frowned. "Dominique? The only one I know by that name died in that car accident in 1933." Shannon's eyes widened. "Wait. What?"

"I swear I'm not losing it. I saw her ghost. I tried to tell myself I was dreaming, but it was no dream."

"There's no such thing as ghosts."

"Tell that to Dominique." Charli shook her head. "I don't

mean to be snarky. I'm still shook up. The woman from the newspaper clipping spoke to me. She was wearing the same dress she had on in that photo. It was torn and bloody, like she'd been in an accident."

Shannon glanced around. "This place is really haunted? The rumors are true?"

Charli drank more tea. "I don't know what to believe. We are awake, right?"

"I'm awake," Shannon answered. "Did Dominique talk? What did she say?"

"She wants us to help find who killed Louise."

"She doesn't know?" Shannon leaned in and whispered, "Aren't ghosts supposed to go through walls and see everything?"

Charli laughed softly. "She and Andre were in Purgatory when Louise was killed."

"Purgatory?"

"She called it the holding place. Dominique also wants us to discover if Andre's brother Maurice murdered them by cutting the brakes on their car. He had gambling debts, and when their father died, Andre inherited a larger share of the estate. With him gone, Maurice got more."

"Holy crap!"

Charli wrapped her hands around the warm mug. "She said something else that was a little strange."

"Like everything you just told me isn't weird?"

"I know. I'm still shook up. She said she and Andre are here to help Travis and me find our destiny."

"Destiny? That sounds very intriguing, like you and Travis are meant for each other. Wow! Matchmaking ghosts."

"It's all too much to absorb. I asked Dominique about the tower key. They don't know where it is. Dominique suggested we search the wine cellar. Louise spent a lot of time there, and they think she took the key from Jeanne after she died."

Shannon slid back. "Double holy crap! Dominique and

Andre aren't as helpful as I would have imagined ghosts would be."

Charli finished her tea and pushed aside her mug. "Let's check the wine cellar now, and find a nice bottle to drink. I need it."

<><><>

Andre leaned against the kitchen doorframe as the women passed through him. He nodded toward Dominique on her favorite perch, the kitchen counter.

"You didn't send Charli screaming out of here when you appeared to her. Well done, ma cherie, but I don't like you using more of your essence."

"I will be okay. Charli is a Deveraux. Of course, she didn't run out of here. She's strong." Dominique floated to the floor. "Let's go with them."

A loud meow made her look down. "You may come with us, mon Ange."

<><><>

"Where to start?" Shannon asked when she and Charli got to the cellar.

Hands on hips, Charli surveyed the room. The dim light from the hanging bulb threw shadows on the brick walls. Terra-cotta slots, each holding a bottle of wine, lined three walls and stretched to the ceiling. She shivered with the cold.

"First, let's pick out something for dinner tonight." Charli perused the shelves. She pulled out a bottle, blew dust off it, and read the label. "A 1982 Chateau Lafite Rothschild. This thing's got to be worth a fortune. I hope we haven't drunk all the lower brands. I don't want to open the valuable stuff."

"You don't want to take any of this wine to Philly?"

"Too much trouble and expense." Charli set the Chateau Lafite Rothschild back into its slot and pulled out another bottle to read the label. "Local, from the shop in the village. This will do for dinner." Setting the bottle on the tasting table, she glanced up. "I need to put in a brighter bulb here. It's hard to see into the corners. There's a lot more to do with the manor than I'd originally thought. I'll never get it all done in the week we have left. I need to extend my leave at work."

"Do you really want to go back to that job?"

Charli sank into one of the chairs that surrounded the table. Her mind jumbled with decisions and all the work involved in selling the house. Then there was Travis. Her growing feelings for him complicated things.

Exhaling, she focused on Shannon. "I've been asking myself the same question. I don't want to go back to that soulless job, but I'm scared. My parents always told me not to give up a sure thing. The bank is a sure thing. Mom and Dad were happy and in love but neither of them took chances. They always did what was expected of them. I'm the same."

Arms folded across her chest, Shannon relaxed against an exposed section of brick wall. "You don't have to be like your parents. I know they were good people and you loved them, but you need to do what's right for you, what you want. What do you want, Charli? From what you make for the house and grounds, and from the sale of this wine, you can quit your job and buy into Chloe's gallery. You've been given a second chance. Take it."

"A second chance to do it right." Charli shrugged. "Or make new mistakes."

"Everyone makes mistakes. It's how we learn. Don't let that stop you from snatching the life you want. What about Travis?" Shannon added quietly.

"That puts another spin on things. I'm beginning to care for him, but…"

"But, what?"

"Am I falling for Travis because I have genuine feelings for him or because he's roused my sexuality? I've never felt this passion before, but I'm so inexperienced, what do I know?"

Shannon pulled a chair next to Charli and sat. She took Charli's hand. "We've been friends since our first day at art school. You wouldn't be passionate for a man who meant nothing to you. You and Travis send out vibes. There's something very real and special between you."

"What if he's seducing me because I resemble Louise? He says he never loved her, but maybe he did."

"Stop overthinking everything." Shannon stood. "Let's search for that key."

"I saw some extra lightbulbs in a kitchen drawer. Give me a minute to change out the one in here."

<><><>

"We still have work to do to make Travis and Charli believe they belong together," Dominique said. The ghosts sat on the tasting table listening to the women's conversation.

"They have both been hurt," Andre answered. "It will take a while for them
to trust again, but it will happen. You must believe."

# CHAPTER THIRTY-FOUR

"Where could that key be? We've been through the entire cellar." Charli plucked a wedge of cheese from the tray on the table in the study and slid it into her mouth, washing it down with wine.

The women were enjoying a fire and after-dinner drinks and snacks. They'd exhausted themselves searching the wine cellar. They'd removed and replaced every bottle of wine from its niche, time-consuming, but found no key.

"Dominique said she thinks the key might be in that room?" Shannon poured another glass of the pinot grigio and held out the bottle to Charli. At Charli's nod, she refilled her glass.

"She said Louise spent a lot of time there."

Shannon scanned the room. "Dominique, if you're here, show yourself. I'd love to meet you."

Charli laughed. "I don't think it works that way. They have to be careful not to appear too much or they lose some of their essence."

"What happens if they lose their essence?"

"They stay in the holding place, aka Purgatory, for eternity."

"How sad for them. Although, I'd like to meet her and

Andre."

"I'd already seen Angel, the cat. I thought it was a very realistic dream." Charli nabbed a green olive from the tray and popped it into her mouth.

The doorbell rang, making both women jump.

"I'll answer it." Charli stood and headed to the front door. She peeked through the peephole. Travis. Her pulse spiked. She opened the door to him. Dressed in a black leather jacket, left open, a blue button-down shirt, untucked, faded jeans, and boots, he was more delicious than the cheese tray. And definitely sexier.

Without a word, he cupped her shoulders and drew her to him. He kissed her fervently, hungrily. Moaning softly, she returned his kiss, parting her lips in invitation. Their tongues mated in a passionate dance. Finally, they moved apart.

Her breathing ragged, Charli skimmed a finger over her lips, hot from his kiss. "That's what I call a greeting."

He laughed. "I'd like to greet you that way every day."

"So would I." She slid her arm through his. "Come into the study. Join Shannon and me for some cheese and wine."

With Charli and Travis snuggled together on the sofa, the women filled Travis in on their futile pursuit of the key.

"I can help you hunt for it," he said. "Charli, you need to get into that room before you sell this place in case there's anything valuable. Maybe we'll find clues to who killed Louise, too." He took a cracker from the tray and bit down on it. "What made you search the wine cellar?"

Charli and Shannon exchanged looks.

"What?" He swung his attention between the women.

"Tell him," Shannon said.

He looked expectantly at Charli. "Tell me what?"

Stalling for time to gather her words, Charli refilled her glass. "Dominique Deveraux suggested we explore the cellar. She said Louise spent a lot of time there."

He dropped the remainder of his cracker. "Dominque Deveraux? She died in the Thirties."

"That's the one," Charli said.

Travis set down his glass and slowly faced Charli. "You're telling me you spoke with a person who's been dead over eighty years?"

"She sees dead people," Shannon said with a laugh. "Like the movie."

"I saw her ghost," Charli said. "I liked her. She and Andre want to find out who killed Louise, too. She also asked me to find evidence Andre's brother Maurice cut the brakes on their car, which caused the accident that killed them." She didn't tell him about the spirits wanting to help them embrace their destiny.

"You lost me at 'ghost'." Travis lifted his glass and tossed back the rest of his drink, then poured another from the second bottle Shannon had set in front of him. "You're level-headed women. I believe you. Louise told me stories of seeing and hearing spirits. Why do the ghosts want to help find Louise's killer?"

"They're on a mission from God."

"I'm going to need something stronger than wine." Confusion flashed across Travis's face. "If they're ghosts, shouldn't they have seen Louise murdered?"

Charli shook her head. "At the time of Louise's death, Dominique and Andre were in what she called the holding place, and which I call Purgatory. But she admitted they'd been around here for a few decades haunting places and people until they went to the light."

He shoved a hand through his hair. "I thought the light took souls to Heaven."

"Sometimes it takes them to Purgatory."

"Okay. I'm afraid to learn more."

They sat for a while discussing strategy for doing a thorough search of the manor, then Shannon left to go to her room to work.

Alone with Travis, Charli leaned into him. He put his arm around her shoulders. The dying embers of the fire glowed in the shadowed room. The wind had kicked up, signaling another storm. Peace settled over Charli like a warm coat.

"This is enjoyable," she said. "Sitting before a fire in a cozy room while the wind screams outside. I can forget lost keys, manor houses, and ghosts."

He kissed the top of her head. "What's enjoyable is being close to you."

She pulled away and stared into his eyes. "I missed you last night."

He swept strands of hair away from her face with gentle fingers. "I missed you too. I worried about you and had to come over. I never figured you'd be talking to ghosts. I should stay here for a while to be sure you're safe. From humans, not ghosts."

Needing him, wanting him, she swayed toward him. His hot gaze spread blazing heat through her.

"Charli," he whispered, his voice harsh with need.

Then his lips were on hers, scorching her.

Charli linked her arms around his neck and leaned back on the sofa, Travis over her. Rubbing herself against him, she savored the sensation of his taut body. His erection, hard against her stomach, fueled her desperate craving for him.

A flash of lightning illuminated the room, followed by the crack of thunder. Charli pressed closer to Travis. The storm outside rivaled the storm of passion that flowed through her veins.

His lips claimed her as he slid his fingers into her hair. Low moans escaped her. He lifted his head. In the dim light, his eyes glazed with desire.

"Let's go to bed." He stood and held out a hand to her, helping her up.

Arm-in-arm, they went up the stairs to her bedroom and a night made for love.

# CHAPTER THIRTY-FIVE

*P*ale fingers of dawn reached into the bedroom and caressed Travis, waking him. Raising himself up on one elbow, he looked down at Charli sleeping peacefully next to him. He smiled at the vulnerability on her beautiful face. Why did he ever think she favored Louise? Charli glowed with an inner beauty the other woman never possessed.

He reached out a hand to skim fingers along her satin-smooth skin, then withdrew. He didn't want to wake her. Hands behind his head, he lay back and stared at the ceiling. He chuckled. He'd kept her busy for hours. She needed her rest.

The question he'd avoided for weeks rose to the surface. What was he doing with Charli? She'd leave soon to return to her real life.

Regret pounded his chest. He didn't want her to go, and he didn't want to hurt her, but he had no right to ask her to stay. Yet, he couldn't keep away from her. She made him happy. No other woman had ever made him crave to be near her, to touch her, laugh with her. Maybe he was falling in love for the first time in his life. The thought scared him to death.

He'd never needed anyone before. Sent to boarding school by

his workaholic father and globe-trotting mother when he was eight, he'd learned early to depend only on himself. He didn't want to need Charli. He'd had his share of women before Charli, but with each one, including Louise, he held a part of himself back. He wanted to give his all to Charli.

Remembering their wild lovemaking, he smiled. Charli had told him she wasn't sexually experienced, but she responded to him with an eagerness and willingness to learn that excited him. A disturbing thought intruded. Perhaps she cared for him because he'd awakened her sexually. Once they parted, he'd be a pleasant memory. She'd find another man to take his place. His stomach clenched as he pictured Charli making love with someone else, laughing with another man, making another man happy.

"Travis?" Her sexy voice, thick with sleep, drew him from his dark musings. He turned to her and gathered her to him, kissing her waiting lips.

"You should go back to sleep," he said. "I didn't allow you to get much rest last night."

She rubbed against him, provoking a groan from him. "The best reason in the world to lose sleep. Love me again."

<><><>

The ghosts sat in the study. In the dawn, the household was silent.

"Mon amour, will Charli and Travis discover it is their destiny to be together, as it was ours?" Dominique asked.

"Their love will heal them and fulfill our mission."

Dominique put her hand on his arm. "It is more important they find the happiness they deserve than we go to the good place. If we have to lose all our essence and spend eternity in the holding place, it will be worth it to bring Charli and Travis together."

Andre froze, then smiled. "I think we are learning the meaning of putting others before ourselves. Perhaps that is the lesson God wanted to teach us all along."

<><><>

The sun had fully risen when Travis and Charli made their way to the kitchen for breakfast. The quiet meant Shannon still slept.

Charli yawned. Although sleep-deprived, her body sang with contentment and sexual energy. She grabbed Travis's hand and stood on tiptoe to kiss his cheek.

"What was that for?" he asked.

"Thanks for last night." Her face heated and she knew she blushed. "And this morning. And for making me feel wanted and precious."

He ran his hands down her arms to her fingertips. "Thank *you*." With a playful grin, he pulled her closer. "I will always want you. You will always be precious to me. Let's go back to bed."

Laughing, she put a hand on his chest. "Down, boy. I'm hungry."

He kissed her tenderly and cupped her face between his hands. "I'm hungry for you."

Yearning coursed through her. Her excitement for this man terrified and excited her. She stepped back. "I want nothing more than to spend the day in bed with you, but there's work to do. You make the coffee and I'll fix some omelets."

"Oui, patronne!" he said, using the French word for boss.

Laughing, Charli strode to the refrigerator and began pulling out ingredients for the omelets. Happiness colored her world. She'd enjoy every minute with Travis. She would not imagine the future.

They were finishing their meal when Shannon, dressed in jeans and a Philadelphia Eagles T-shirt, bopped into the room.

"The smell of that coffee woke me." Stifling a yawn, she ambled to the coffee maker and poured herself a cup.

Leaning against the counter, she nodded to the others. "You two were up early."

Travis raised his coffee mug to his mouth, hiding his grin. Heat rode Charli's cheeks.

"Busy day ahead." Charli stood. "I'd better get my shower."

"I should take one, too." Travis threw down his napkin and followed Charli from the room.

"Have fun, you two," Shannon called after them.

In Charli's room, Travis pulled her to him and backed her up to the closed door. He kissed her mouth and nibbled his way down her throat. "You're more delicious than any food."

His lips left a trail of fire on her flesh. She gripped his shoulders. "We were rude to Shannon." Her voice trembled.

"Do you think she cares?" he rasped against her throat.

"No." Charli knew Shannon would understand and be happy for her. Shannon had always been more sexually experienced than Charli. Funny how life had a way of balancing things.

Travis pulled away. The gleam in his eyes sparked something deep and pulsing within Charli.

"Into the shower with you," he growled.

<><><>

Shannon, Travis, and Charli combed the manor methodically, starting with the top floor. They checked for loose floorboards, they opened drawers, bent to peek under furniture.

In the kitchen, having a late lunch of ham sandwiches and soup, Charli ran a hand over her hair. Frustration tightened her chest.

"It's useless," she said. "I give up. Let's call in a locksmith to open the tower door and hope he doesn't damage it too much. I don't like bringing in a stranger to open that room. The less people who know what we're up to, the better."

Travis, sitting next to her, put his hand over hers. "Let's finish our search. If we come up empty, we bring in a locksmith."

<><><>

"I feel strongly the key is here," Dominque said.

Angel washed herself while Dominique and Andre searched the cellar again.

"We've been all over this place. So have the others." Andre's gaze swung through the room. He froze. "Does that brick seem odd?" He pointed to a brick protruding a miniscule amount from the wall.

"We never noticed that before."

"It's easy to miss." Andre raised his eyes to the single light fixture. "Charli replaced the bulb with a brighter one. See how the light shines on the wall."

He and Dominique hurried over and knelt to examine the brick. He tried to pry the brick off, but to no avail.

"I cannot loosen it. You must tell Charli," he said. "She will know what to do."

# CHAPTER THIRTY-SIX

Charli reached across the kitchen peninsula for the wine. The bottle fell sideways, surprising Charli. Cold wine covered the counter. She jumped up and stopped the rolling bottle before it plunged to the floor.

"Odd," she said. "How did that happen?"

Travis grabbed napkins and began wiping the counter. Shannon ran to peel off paper towels.

"Charli!" The whispered word made Charli look to the doorway. Her heart pounded.

Dominique stood there, beckoning with her finger for Charli to follow her. Charli looked at Travis and Shannon. They were busy cleaning the countertop and didn't appear to have heard or seen Dominique.

Charli followed Dominique from the room. "What is it?" she asked the ghost in a shaky voice. "Why can't the others see you?"

"Bonjour, Charli." The ghost smiled. "We spirits determine who can see us, but there are those mortals with enhanced psychic powers who see us even if we don't want them to. Enough about that. I have what I think is good news."

Charli clenched her hands at her sides. "You've really got to stop sneaking up on me like this."

"I did not sneak."

"Wait. Did you knock that bottle down?"

"Not I, but Andre."

"Never mind. What did you have to tell me?"

"Andre and I might have found the key to the tower."

"You did? Where is it?"

"Perhaps behind a brick in the wine cellar. We cannot pry it open but you can, especially that strong hunk Travis."

"We didn't notice anything that indicated a hiding place."

"You put that new bulb in and the room is brighter. Follow the light and explore close to the floor."

"Thanks, Dominique." She went back into the kitchen and stopped in the doorway.

Shannon and Travis turned to her with questioning expressions.

Travis went to her. "Are you okay? You look shaken. Don't worry about the spilled wine."

"I'm not worried about that. I think I know where the key to the tower is."

"You do?" Shannon jumped off her stool. "Where?"

"To the wine cellar." Charli headed out, the others close behind.

In the cellar, she turned on the bulb that hung over the tasting table. "Follow the light, close to the floor," she repeated like a mantra.

"What are you doing?" Travis asked.

On her knees, Charli examined the brick wall where the light touched it. "Aha!"

The others squatted down next to her.

"What are we looking at?" Shannon asked.

Charli crouched lower and pointed to the oddly angled brick. "That."

189

"Let me try to force it open." Travis pushed at the brick with his hands but it didn't budge.

"I'll find something." Looking around, Charli spotted a heavy wine opener on the table. She jumped up, snatched it, and brought it to Travis.

Using the opener, he pried the brick loose, then felt around in the opening. A triumphant look on his face, he held up a key.

"Woo hoo!" Charli snatched the key from his fingers. "Let's go."

The three of them raced up the stairs to the third floor. When they reached the tower door, Charli braced one arm against the wall, breathing heavily.

She gave Travis a narrow-eyed glare. "You're not even winded."

He winked. "I exercise."

Her face burned. Charli knew what kind of exercise he excelled at.

He laughed softly. "Ready to find what's behind the door?"

"I hope we're not opening a Pandora's Box." Charli's insides shook as she inserted the key into the old-fashioned lock. The key slid in easily and she turned it. The lock clicked. Relief made her dizzy, and she stepped back.

Travis wound his arm around her waist. "You okay?"

She swallowed. "I can't believe we're in."

Feeling like Nancy Drew, girl detective, triumph mixed with anxiety as Charli slowly pulled the door open. Creaking on its metal hinges, it opened toward them to reveal a set of narrow stairs.

"Dracula's castle," Shannon said.

Charli wrinkled her nose. "Enough with Dracula."

"We have to go up one at a time," Travis said. "Better let me go first." He went cautiously up the stairs, the women following.

The stairs led directly to the turret room.

Charli peeked from behind Travis. "Thank God there's not another door here."

Travis stepped into the room, Charli and Shannon close behind.

In the room, Charli blinked. Dominique waved from her spot on a steamer trunk. A handsome man who resembled Charli's father, dressed in Thirties clothes, the pants torn and bloody, stood next to her. Angel twined around the man's ankles.

Seeing Andre provoked a surge of sadness and nostalgia that clutched her stomach. She wished desperately her parents were here to experience Deveraux Manor.

Travis cupped her elbow. "You sure you're okay? You're white as those sheets covering the furniture."

She was glad he didn't compare her to a ghost. "I'm good. Can't believe we're actually in this room."

"What made you recheck the cellar?" Shannon asked.

"A hunch." Although she'd told the others about the ghosts, Charli didn't want to talk about them with the spirits so close and hanging on her every word.

Shannon frowned but kept quiet.

In a quick sweep, Charli took stock. She estimated the round room to be thirty feet in circumference. Six long narrow windows took up one side. On one wall hung a print of Van Gogh's The Starry Night. A medieval tapestry graced the wall opposite the doorway. An Oriental rug in shades of blue covered most of the dark hardwood floor. Large steamer trunks with travel stickers from foreign countries were set before the tapestry. Under the windows, smaller trunks and wooden chests of drawers were arranged. Sheets outlined the shapes of a chaise lounge and chairs near the center of the room.

"That tapestry is amazing. The colors jump out." Charli pointed to the wall hanging depicting a knight on horseback fighting a dragon. "I wonder if that's St. George." She walked to the tapestry and ran her hands over it. "This may pre-date St.

George. Depending on the age, it could be worth a lot of money. I'll take a closer look later. We can bring in an expert to assess it."

"I never knew a time when that wall hanging wasn't there," Andre said. "I never paid it much attention."

"There's so much here." Charli made a beeline for the framed paintings that leaned against the wall where the Van Gogh hung. She ran her hands over an oil painting of Dominque and Andre lounging against their red sports car, probably the one in which they'd been killed.

"So beautiful," she whispered. "Both of you."

The spirits came to stand beside her, their arms entwined.

Dominique sniffed. "Andre and I were the most beautiful couple in Deveraux."

"In all of France," he answered, his voice rough.

"What do you have there?" Travis walked through the ghosts. He shivered and rubbed his arms. "There's a draft here somewhere."

Charli swallowed. "It's not a draft. You walked through the spirits."

Travis froze and turned around. "What? They're here? Why can't we see them?"

"They have to be careful not to lose too much of their essence. They control who sees them."

He blew out a breath. "Okay. All that takes a little getting used to."

"I get how you feel," Shannon said.

Charli didn't want to talk about the ghosts. "Travis, help me with this painting. I want to bring it downstairs."

He picked up the painting and examined it. "Dominique and Andre Deveraux. I recognize them from the newspaper article. The work was done by a talented artist. It has some damage from being here in all sorts of temperatures. I can fix it so it's like new."

Charli blinked back tears and raised her eyes to his. "Thank you. I'll take this to Philadelphia, to remember Dominique, Andre, and Angel."

"Hey, look at this." Shannon stood next to an opened trunk and held up a pink feather boa.

Charli laughed. "Wonder who wore that?"

"It wasn't me." Dominique's face twisted in displeasure. "*Sans classe*. I believe that *thing* belonged to Louise."

Stifling a laugh, Charli sauntered over to the trunk and bent to poke around at the contents. "Looks like a bunch of old clothes here."

"Old clothes!" Dominique huffed. "Mon Dieu! My clothes were couture. I would wear nothing less."

Andre pulled his wife against him. "Come, it is time to leave. You are getting upset."

The ghosts disappeared in a flash.

Charli straightened and hugged herself, missing them.

Travis opened another trunk and sat on his haunches to dig through it. "Lots of old books in this one."

"Let's go through the smaller trunks and the chests as best we can now. See if there's anything of value." Charli marched to one of the chests.

They searched for close to two hours, but found nothing valuable, mostly clothes, table linens, and books. The old photos in frames interested Charli, and she thought she'd take them back to Philadelphia.

"I'm exhausted." Charli pulled her hair into a ponytail, releasing it to fall over her shoulders. "I hoped we'd find a safe, but I guess not."

"Not yet," Travis said.

Charli headed to one of the steamer trunks and touched the cracked canvas. "Louis Vuitton. These aren't in great shape, but if they're authentic Louis V, they're worth a pretty penny."

Travis stood next to her. "I'll unlatch it." He opened the trunk, which had been stored upright, to expose a set of drawers on one side and a section closed with a leather flap opposite. The faint scent of lavender wafted from the trunk.

Charli slid open a drawer. "Wow! Look at all this Art Deco jewelry. I've bought some of this at flea markets, but nothing so spectacular." She pulled out a rhinestone brooch. "This is lovely." The oval-shaped pin of about two inches was set with emerald-cut and round rhinestones. Charli turned it over. "I've seen one like this before. The brooch separates into two clips."

"Cool!" Shannon took the brooch from her and admired it. "Beautiful." She set it back in the drawer. "Plenty of amazing jewelry here, but no ruby or diamond and pearl necklaces."

Charli pushed aside the flap on the other side. "Look at this. Dresses. Colorful. Beautiful. On these hangers. I assume these have been here a long time, but they appear to be in good shape."

"Might be too much to examine now," Travis said. "It's late, and we've been at this a while."

"I agree." Charli turned to him. "Why don't you stay over? Being in this room might jog your memory about something Jeanne or Louise said. If you're here, we can get an early start in the morning."

He placed a tender kiss on her lips. "I'll stay."

Shannon rolled her eyes. "You two don't fool me. Of course, he planned to stay."

Charli threw the feather boa at her.

Laughing, they exited the room and went single-file down the stairs. Charli locked the door and slipped the key into her jeans pocket. She shivered at the strong feeling of premonition that traveled through her.

# CHAPTER THIRTY-SEVEN

*T*ravis slowly opened his eyes. Charli's warm body snuggled against him. Contentment he hadn't known in years surged through him. She'd touched his soul, made him believe in goodness again. He wished he could remember something about the turret room that would help her.

Like a delicate paint stroke on canvas, fear touched his heart. She had a life away from Normandy. She'd made it clear she'd leave once she put the manor on the market. He had no right to hold her here. He wanted her to stay, or to ask him to go with her. She had to want him, and only him.

Travis turned onto his side to watch her, his angel with kitten claws. Her dark hair spread out on the white pillow. Thick black lashes fanned her high cheekbones. Her full lips were swollen from his kisses.

He had to have her again. He smoothed hair back from her face, then kissed her sweet throat. She stirred and opened her beautiful eyes.

"'Morning," she murmured.

He caressed the satiny skin of her face. "I want to love you again."

<><><>

Later, after a quick breakfast, Shannon, Travis, and Charli trudged up to the third floor to the tower and the turret room. Charli carried a flashlight to shine into the dark corners. By late afternoon, they'd combed through the Louis V trunks to discover beautiful gowns and dresses and more high-quality costume jewelry. Air-tight boxes contained shoes and purses, the leather cracked on most. Some of the luggage and contents of the trunks held value, but not enough to warrant keeping the door locked.

Tired, Charli sat on one of the smaller trunks. They'd put back all the clothes, careful not to damage the exquisite fabrics. Later, she'd go through the dresses and study the faded labels, taking inventory. She hadn't seen the ghosts since yesterday. She'd figured they'd want to be in the room when they searched, but maybe seeing Charli and the others go through their belongings proved too much for them. If only the spirits had been around to see who killed Louise.

Travis paced the room with narrowed eyes, taking his time. He stopped and pivoted to the wall opposite the bank of windows. Charli followed his gaze to the print of the Van Gogh. Late sunshine highlighted the pale blue and yellow of the painting.

"I wonder." Travis frowned, his focus on the Van Gogh.

"What is it?" Charli pushed up from the trunk.

Shannon turned from the windows.

All three strode to the Van Gogh.

Travis ran his fingers over the print. "In movies, safes are always hidden behind a painting. There was so much to see here yesterday, I barely paid attention to this print. Something about it bothered me, and now I think I know what it is." Using both hands, he tugged on the frame, but it wouldn't loosen. He felt along the sides. A small click, then the painting swung open to reveal a safe recessed into the wall. "I'll be damned."

Charli blinked, not believing her eyes. "Oh, my God."

"There has to be something valuable in there," Shannon said. "Or clues to Louise's murder. Or both."

"There might not be anything of value." Charli shrugged.

Travis pulled on the safe's handle but the door didn't budge. He turned the combination lock, but it remained closed. "We'll never figure out the combination."

"What do we do now?" Charli asked. "Unless you have a safe cracker on retainer."

Shaking his head, Travis turned to her. "No. Wish I knew some shady people."

Shannon held out her hands. "How are we going to get this opened?"

"The locksmith who was here the other day might be able to open this," Travis said.

Charli folded her arms across her chest. "If he can, will he be discreet? We don't want the whole town to know about the safe in case there is something a thief would break in for."

Travis raked fingers through his hair. "If I pay the locksmith enough, he'll keep quiet."

"I'll pay." Charli raised her chin to meet his eyes.

"It's liable to be expensive. I'm invested in finding what the thing holds." Travis tucked strands of Charli's hair behind her ear. "You've got enough worries. Let me handle this for you."

Shannon glanced out the windows and back to the others. "The sun is setting. I doubt we can get a locksmith out here today."

"Nothing more we can do now," Travis said. "We need a break. I'll take you both to dinner tonight at a small café in the village. Good food." He nodded to Charli. "Okay?"

"Okay."

"We'll swing by Beliveau to see if Max wants to come to dinner with us, and I'll pack a change of clothes. Max might give us advice on breaking into that safe. He used to be MI6."

"Max was a spy?" both women said in unison.

Travis smiled. "Don't tell him I told you. Max prefers not to talk about his previous life."

Charli rubbed a hand over her forehead. Murders, ghosts, spies, missing jewels, a hidden safe, a man she cared for.

*You're not in Kansas anymore!*

# CHAPTER THIRTY-EIGHT

*T*he next morning after breakfast, Charli and Travis headed to the stairs to go to her room to shower and change. A knock sounded at the front door, stopping them. They exchanged frowns.

"I'll get it." Travis gestured for Charli to wait.

He opened the door to Max, who carried a duffel bag.

"'Morning, Max." Charli smiled at the older man.

He stepped inside and dropped the duffels. "I decided to take you up on your offer at dinner last night to stay here for a few days in case you need help and extra protection once the safe is opened."

"We appreciate it, and you're always welcome here." Truth be told, Charli felt safer with both men there and was glad Max had accepted her invitation.

She saw Max's barrel chest and military bearing in a new light. His lined face spoke of a life spent in the shadows. A shiver went up her spine.

"I'll show you to your room," she said.

Max nodded. "I'll put my things in the room, but I'll be sleeping down here in case someone tries to break in."

"I hope no one tries to break in, but you can sleep on the sofa in the study if you want. You'll be more comfortable in a bed."

"I know best how to protect you."

"Oo-kay, then."

Max followed Travis and Charli up the stairs. "The vault specialist is coming over later today."

Travis stopped and turned to him. "You called a vault specialist?"

"Ordinary locksmiths can't open safes. You need someone specially trained. The man I hired is one of the best in the business. And he's discreet. I've used him in the past."

Charli looked over her shoulder at Max. "I've never heard of a vault specialist. Is he from around here?"

"He is from Paris, among other places."

Charli showed Max to his room and tried to sort out her tangled thoughts. Things were getting stranger and stranger. Now, a safecracker, rather vault specialist, who might have a shady past would intrude into her life.

After Max put his bag in the bedroom, he and Travis set about double checking the interior of the house for any vulnerable areas. Charli thought they were being overly cautious, but Deveraux Village was a small place, and if they found anything valuable in the safe, word could get out.

While the men busied themselves, Shannon worked in her room. Charli decided to go through the items in the Louis V steamers. She'd catalogued most of what she'd found in the house that had value. She wanted to make a list of what the trunks contained. The sooner she determined what objects deserved selling and which she could give away, the sooner she could put the house on the market.

Or not.

She froze on her way to the third-floor stairs. Where had that thought come from? She could stay here, but how would she support herself if she didn't sell the house? She barely spoke

French, so couldn't work here. She was being fanciful and foolish, so unlike her. She never made rash decisions.

With the money she made on the sale of the house and its contents, she'd quit her job and buy into Chloe's gallery. She should quit her job now. Decisions jumbled in her head, giving her the beginnings of a headache.

Once back to her life in Philadelphia, Travis would be a sweet memory. She swallowed the sudden lump that formed in her throat. She didn't want him to be merely a memory.

Pushing the thought away, she headed to the turret, paper and pen in hand. She also took a magnifying glass she found in a desk drawer, to help her read the faded labels on the dresses.

In the turret, she set her supplies on the floor and went to one of the trunks. A black gown that appeared to be the only dress in the chest was folded over several hangers and covered with tissue paper. She pulled the gown out, then stood and held the dress up to better examine it. Stunning, lace trimmed the scoop neckline and cap sleeves. Ruffles of matching lace started halfway down the black silk to the hemline.

The beauty and artistry of the dress touched her soul. "Magnificent," she whispered.

She scooped up the magnifying glass and put it to the label. She gasped and almost dropped the dress. "Chanel! Oh. My. God."

"I loved that dress."

At the soft feminine voice, Charli released a small scream that was more of a squeak and whirled around. Dominique and Andre, Angel at their feet, stood behind her.

"This was yours?" Charli asked Dominique.

"But, of course." Dominique pulled a floral silk dress from another trunk and held it up to her. She twirled around. "Remember this, Andre?"

"Ma cherie, you were beautiful in that dress. I loved taking you dancing in it." He grinned. "I loved taking it off you later."

"You are so sexy." Dominique kissed him on the cheek.

Uncomfortable with sex talk from spirits, Charli cleared her throat to get their attention. "Please don't sneak up on me like that again. You gave me a fright."

Andre laughed and held out his hands. "We are ghosts, non? We are supposed to scare everyone." He bowed slightly. "We have not been properly introduced. I am Andre, your grandfather's brother." He tilted his head to study her. "Yes, you are a Deveraux."

"Nice to meet you, Andre." Now, she was having polite conversation with spirits.

"Where have you been?" Charli asked. "We could have used some help yesterday when we went through this room."

Angel meowed, and Dominique dropped the floral dress back into the trunk and picked up the cat. She stroked the pet's fluffy white fur and smiled at Charli. "I became too upset seeing all my wonderful clothes and jewelry. Andre and I had to leave."

Charli studied them. "Is it my imagination, or are you both a bit transparent? I couldn't see through you before."

"We have lost some of our essence."

"You shouldn't take the chance on losing all your essence."

Andre waved his hand. "Non. It is okay."

"A vault." Dominique nodded toward the wall where the safe was exposed.

"You didn't know about the safe?" Charli asked.

The spirits shook their heads.

"Maurice, Jeanne, or Louise must have had it installed after our unfortunate demise," Andre said. "We had no safe when I lived."

Dominique shuddered. "After we left the mortal world, we were in that—that place for some years and did not know what was happening here."

"I'd hoped you had the combination. A specialist is coming over later. Fingers crossed, he can open it." Charli gestured with her arm to take in the room. "In the meantime, I'd like you to help me sort through some of this, but you might use up too much of your essence."

"We have told you not to worry about that."

"Okay, but I can't help worrying. Maybe this will go quickly. I don't know what's valuable that I should sell and what I should give away."

Dominique huffed, looking insulted. "All my clothes are of value."

Ghosts could be so difficult. "The clothes are beautiful," Charli said. "Old clothes don't bring a lot of money unless they're couture." She held up the black gown. "Like this Chanel."

"Do you think I would wear anything other than couture?" Dominque narrowed her eyes at Charli.

"Ma cherie, calm down," Andre said.

Dominique set a protesting Angel on the floor. "Come, I will help. Most of my dresses are Balenciaga and Chanel." She smiled and turned to Andre. "Remember those yacht parties we went to with Coco?"

He grinned. "Coco could party."

Charli widened her eyes. "You mean Coco Chanel?"

"But of course. Who else?" Dominique said.

Charli took a closer look at the trunks holding the dresses and gowns. Excitement made her pulse beat double-time. "This room might hold a small fortune in clothes alone. I wonder why Jeanne or Louise never sold them."

Andre shrugged. "Perhaps they did not want to part with them, or planned to sell them at a future time."

"Could be," Charli said. "What other designer dresses are here?"

Dominque pointed to the flowered dress she'd held up. "That is a Schiaparelli." She laughed. "That Elsa Schiaparelli loved her wine. There are some Lanvins, a Patou or two. There's an old Poiret that Andre's mother wore."

"Paul Poiret?" Charli sank to the floor.

"You've heard of him?" Dominique asked.

"His dresses are works of art. I took a class on him and the other classic designers when I was in art college." Charli took shallow breaths. "I need to contact a fashion curator. I wouldn't know the first thing about selling these."

Dominque lifted the flowered Schiaparelli and held it close. "It still has my perfume." Tears filled her eyes.

Andre gathered her to him. "It is all going to be okay. Charli will make sure your clothes are handled with love."

# CHAPTER THIRTY-NINE

*B*y dinnertime, the vault specialist hadn't shown. He'd called Max to say he'd gotten held up on a job outside Paris and would be there as soon as he could.

Charli was exhausted from handling so many delicate pieces of clothing. Beautiful, priceless gowns and dresses that took special care when touching. The sale of the garments alone might bring the money she needed to buy into the gallery. Finding those clothes was the tipping point that broke through the dam of her indecision.

She needed to stay longer in France to get expert advice on selling the clothes, the wine, and the other artifacts in the turret room. She'd give notice at work. Never going back to her soul-sucking job made her feel lighter than she had in years.

Being with Travis made her happier than she'd been in her life.

Shannon, Charli, Travis, and Max had a light supper while waiting for the vault man, as Charli referred to him. The spirits had agreed to stay around to watch the safe opened. They were as curious about the contents as Charli. They'd disappeared and

Charli assumed they were still there, but conserving their essences.

Shannon grinned. "I'm excited about all that vintage couture and the gorgeous costume jewelry."

"My mind is blown." Charli sipped her wine. "I'm reeling from the treasure hidden in the room, including that amazing tapestry. I never thought I'd see, let alone own, such exquisite items."

"I suspect there are attics in France holding small fortunes in designer clothes and other works of art," Travis said.

"How so?" Shannon asked.

"What wasn't looted by the Nazis during the Occupation was well-hidden."

Charli pushed aside her empty plate. "I never thought of that."

The doorbell rang. Max stood quickly. "Probably the vault specialist. You three stay here until I tell you it's okay."

Shannon's gaze followed him out of the room. "I feel like he's our babysitter."

Travis slid off his stool. "Max knows what he's doing."

Max, leading a heavyset man holding a large backpack, came into the kitchen. Max gestured to the man. "This is Pierre."

They made their introductions, then headed to the third floor. Charli didn't see the ghosts but felt their presence in the cool air wafting over her. Pierre huffed and puffed up the narrow tower stairs, and Charli feared he wouldn't make it all the way.

In the turret, Pierre set his bag on the floor and examined the safe. The others crowded around him. He said something to Max.

Travis stepped back and Max shooed the women. "He says to give him space."

Charli chewed her lip, watching the man run his fingers over the safe, like a lover caressing his beloved. He put his ear to the door and turned the combination wheel, his expression intense.

He grabbed his bag and pulled out a small foldable stool

which he sat on. Charli was surprised the little seat held him. Dipping his hand back in, he emerged with a stethoscope and a power drill, then said something in French to the group.

Travis turned to Charli. "He says he can use the drill to take out the lock but the safe will be ruined. He can listen to the tumblers to learn the combination, which will preserve the safe, but it might take several hours."

"When they crack a safe in the movies, it takes about fifteen minutes," Shannon said.

"We're not in the movies." Charli met Travis's gaze. "I might need the safe. Plus, it will be a good selling feature. Tell him to take all the time he needs."

Travis relayed the information. Pierre nodded, put on a pair of thick-lensed glasses and leaned in, holding the stethoscope to the steel door. He turned the lock as he listened.

"Charli and Shannon, you don't have to remain here. You probably need a rest," Travis whispered. "We'll stay with him."

Dominique appeared and floated behind Travis. "Andre and I will stay. We trust Travis and Max, but we will keep watch."

"I want to see the safe opened." Despite the ghosts' assurances, Charli wanted to be there. "I need to catalogue these dresses. Shannon and I will do that while your guy works."

"If you are very quiet," Max said. "He needs quiet to hear the tumblers."

"We'll sort them but won't use the computer. I'll bring that up later, and take pictures of the items with my phone. I plan to go online and try to find the dresses so I can gauge their worth."

Charli and Shannon, speaking in whispers, gently sorted through the clothes and separated them by designer, making handwritten notes on the pad Charli had brought up earlier.

Andre appeared. Both ghosts sat on one of the trunks, while Angel sniffed around the room. Andre gestured toward Pierre. "This new technology is good, non?"

Charli nodded, then the ghosts disappeared.

Several hours later, Shannon and Charli, their backs sore from bending over, sat on the chairs they'd uncovered and sipped iced tea. Pierre had taken a short bathroom break and had some iced tea before resuming work. Max refused anything to drink, and leaned stoically against the wall, his arms folded across his chest. Travis, more relaxed, rested on the chaise.

Charli studied Max. She assumed he'd learned rigid self-control while a spy, or was chosen as a spy because of his self-control.

Pierre gave a shout and sat back on his folding stool. Grinning, he turned to the group, his words and face animated.

Travis stood. "He's cracked the lock."

Dominique and Andre re-appeared, along with Angel.

Charli and Shannon put down their drinks and hurried over, crowding around the specialist, along with Max and Travis. This time, Pierre didn't seem to mind. With a triumphant expression, he opened the safe and moved aside for Charli to look in.

Max handed Charli a flashlight.

Her heart rate spiked. She aimed the light inside, illuminating stacks of letters tied with pink ribbons. Nestled in the back, its pink satin cover shining, was a jewel case big enough to hold a necklace. "Oh, my God!"

"What is it?" Shannon leaned over Charli's shoulder and gasped. "Is that what I think it is?"

"What necklace could it be?" Dominique, too, peered over Charli's shoulder.

Closed in, Charli straightened, and Dominique and Shannon moved away. Charli shivered, either from excitement or the ghostly presence. Max might trust the vault specialist, but she didn't want to remove the contents of the safe with him there.

She smiled at Pierre. "Merci."

The specialist handed a piece of paper to Charli.

At Charli's frown, Max, said, "That's the combination."

"Terrific," Charli said. "Thank him again. It's late and I want to take the contents to my room to look over in the morning. How much do we owe him?"

"I'll walk him out. Don't worry about the payment. He owes me a favor."

Charli didn't want to know what kind of favor.

Pierre packed his tools, dipped his head at the others, and followed Max out of the room.

Charli grabbed Travis's hand. "One of the necklaces must be in there. They wouldn't hide an empty case."

Shannon hopped from one foot to another, like an excited child. "Take it out."

Charli released Travis's hand and scooped up the letters, handing them to Shannon. Then, she pulled out the jewel case. "I should open it."

Dominique and Andre hovered over them.

Her hands shaking, Charli opened the box. The ruby and diamond necklace sparkled from its bed of white satin.

At Charli's quick intake of breath, Travis touched her shoulder and squeezed. His touch comforted.

Charli carefully pulled out the necklace and handed the empty box to Travis. She held the jewels up to the dim overhead light. The light caught the facets of the large ruby pendant. Shimmers of red reflected off the beige walls. "This is exquisite. I've never seen anything like it." She turned to the others. "My grandmother Gabrielle didn't steal this, as Jeanne accused. It must be worth a fortune now. We still don't know where the pearl and diamond one is."

Charli took the box from Travis and gently placed the necklace back on its satin bed.

Travis cupped her elbow. "Take everything to your room. You've had a lot of excitement today. Perhaps tomorrow we can go through the letters."

Charli leaned against him. "It's too late for me to try to read anything in French. Maybe we'll find a clue to Louise's murder. And learn if there's more to Jeanne's death."

CHAPTER FORTY

Charli opened her eyes. Darkness filled her bedroom. Something had awakened her. Travis's even breathing as he slept next to her mingled with a foreign sound. She listened carefully. Stealthy footsteps slid over the hardwood floors. Drawers opening spiked her adrenaline. She blinked and sat up. The figure of a man lurked by her dresser. She screamed.

"What the hell?" Travis shot out of bed, flinging the covers away.

The prowler fled.

Charli screamed again. Travis snatched his jeans from a chair and pulled them on as he raced after the intruder. Heavy footsteps pounded the stairs to the third floor.

Charli bolted from the bed and threw on her robe.

Shannon, wild-haired, burst in. "Are you okay? Oh, my God! I saw Max running up the stairs. He had a gun."

"There was someone in my room." Charli's voice shook. "Travis went after him." Charli began to tremble. Afraid her legs wouldn't hold her, she sank onto the bed.

The ghosts glided into the room. Andre pointed a finger

toward the door. "The criminal went to the turret. Max and Travis followed."

"Did you see who it was?" Charli asked.

Shannon glanced around. "Who are you talking to?" Her face paled. "Are they here?"

"Did you see who it was?" Charli asked Andre again.

"Non. He wore a covering on his face, with only the eyes cut out. It was definitely a man. His build was very familiar, tall, muscled."

Dominique nodded. "I thought the same."

Heavy footsteps sounded in the hallway outside Charli's bedroom. She stood and swept her gaze around, searching for something she could use as a weapon.

Max and Travis came into the room, Max holding a gun.

Travis went to Charli and folded her into his arms. "Are you okay?"

"I'm fine, just scared. Did you find him?"

Max put his gun into his waistband. He shook his head. "We searched all the rooms on the third floor, plus the turret room but they were empty."

Charli clutched Travis's arm. "How could that be? The only way out of the third floor is down the stairs. We forgot to lock the tower door, there's no way out through the turret room."

Shannon snapped her fingers. "There could be another set of stairs from that room that lead outside."

Surprise flitted across Travis's face. "What made you think that?"

"Duh. Hidden stairs. That's what happens in horror movies and mystery stories."

Charli tried to laugh, but it fell flat. "Maybe all those creepy shows you're so fond of will pay off."

"I believe you're right about secret stairs," Max said. "That's the only explanation."

"Do you know if he took anything?" Charli asked Travis.

"We couldn't tell. Check to be sure you still have the key to the tower and the contents of the safe."

She went to the dresser, opened a drawer, and dug through her underwear. She waved the key at them. "Still here. I put the necklace and letters under loose floorboards in the closet." She strode to the closet, pushed aside several pairs of shoes, and pried up the floorboards with a metal nail file, then turned to the others. "Everything is here. Thank God I woke up. With more time, he might have found these."

Travis put out his hand. "Let me have the key. I'm going to lock the tower door. We were in too much of a hurry last night. We should have locked it. If there's an outside entrance to the turret, and the intruder comes back, he won't be able to get into the house. Max and I will search the whole place and make sure we're secure before we settle down again."

Max smiled, a rarity for him. "Try to get some sleep, Shannon and Charli. In the morning, we can look through Charli's room to determine if anything was stolen, then we'll find those hidden stairs."

<><><>

Charli woke and stretched. She wanted to cuddle with Travis, but she was alone. The intruder incident pushed into her consciousness, jolting her awake. She sat up. Weak sunlight snaked through the drapes and reflected on the disarray in her room. Clothes were strewn on the floor, tossed there by the prowler. She slid out of bed and snatched up her robe, pulling the sash tightly around her as if she could protect herself from whoever broke in.

"What was he looking for?" she asked the quiet room.

*The contents of the safe.*

Charli whirled around. "My, God, Dominique, you keep

scaring me. Do you think he was looking for the necklace or the letters?"

Andre perched on the dresser next to his wife. "Probably both. Someone knew you'd opened the safe."

Charli rubbed a hand over her forehead where the beginnings of headache pulsed. "Do you know anything about secret stairs in the turret room?"

Andre shook his head. "Non. Many of these ancient homes had hidden rooms and stairs to make an easy escape in times of war." He chuckled. "And to allow lovers to come and go. If Deveraux had such things, they were sealed up long before I was born. No one ever talked about it."

Charli massaged her forehead again. "I can't tackle any of this until I've had coffee." She glanced more closely at the spirits. "You're more transparent than you were the other day. I can see the wall behind you."

Sadness flicked across Dominique's face. "We are losing more of our essence."

"I don't want that to happen to you."

"Do not concern yourself," Andre said. "Our main priority is helping you and Travis."

The ghosts disappeared.

Worried about them, Charli headed to the kitchen where she found the others studying papers spread on the table. Travis ran over to her and took her hand. "Sit. I'll make you something to eat."

While Travis prepared an omelet, Charli poured herself coffee. "You have the blueprints that were in the study? I left them out so I could look at them, but haven't had the chance."

Max raised his head and nodded.

She leaned closer. "Do they show hidden stairs or rooms?"

"No, but I'm not surprised. If they had an escape route, they would have kept it secret."

Shannon rinsed her coffee mug in the sink. "It makes our job a little harder."

Charli and Travis went through her room later. Nothing appeared to be missing. Then, the four of them traipsed up to the turret. All was as they left it the day before. The emptied safe stood open.

Dominique and Andre drifted into the room, then disappeared. Charli knew they were conserving their essence.

"Where do we start?" she asked Shannon.

"Look for anything that seems out of kilter." Shannon smoothed her hands carefully over a section of wall. "These walls are sturdy. No cracks that might indicate a door."

"You really do get into those crazy movies, don't you?" Charli's question provoked a laugh from the others. "Maybe it will work to our advantage now."

"Let me think." Hands on hips, Shannon perused the room. She slapped her forehead. "Of course! How dense are we?"

"What?" Charli asked.

Shannon pointed to the tapestry. "We never peeked behind it. In the movies, hidden rooms and stairs are behind bookcases and wall-hangings."

Charli laughed. "We're not very good sleuths. We missed the safe at first and never thought to look behind the tapestry."

The group hurried over to the wall-hanging of a knight slaying a dragon. Shannon gently pulled part of it aside. Grinning, she turned to the others. "Looks like we might have a door back here."

Max swiped a hand over his short hair. "I'll be damned."

Travis folded the tapestry back farther, exposing the outline of a door without a handle. He leaned against the door and pushed with his shoulder. It opened quietly. "Someone oiled the hinges."

Charli peeked past him. "Steps."

Max pushed more of the tapestry aside and shone his flashlight into the darkness. "No cobwebs. Someone's been here recently."

Charli gripped Travis's arm. "Let's go down."

"I'll go first," he said. Max handed him the flashlight.

Max went next, followed by the women.

A cool draft blew over Charli, and she knew the spirits were with them.

A nervous laugh escaped Charli. "Nancy Drew and the Hardy Boys in The Great Turret Mystery."

Travis twisted to look at her. "What?"

"Private joke."

The steps were steep and narrow, made of stone, and looked as if they'd been hollowed out of the ground. They ended at an ancient-looking wooden door. Travis pulled on the metal handle, and the door swung inward.

He turned back to the others. "We need to go out one-by-one. There's just enough space cleared between the bushes for one person to stand."

Single-file, they stepped into a tiny clearing. Travis held back the shrubberies on one side, creating a narrow path for the others. Free of the greeneries, the group turned toward the house.

The ghosts, holding hands, appeared again. Andre left Dominique for a closer look. He turned to her. "Why did we not know this?"

She shrugged. "Everyone who knew had died."

Charli blinked in the sunlight. They were on the right of the house. Thick foliage hid the door from view. "Whoever got in must have made the crude opening by cutting through the vegetation. With the heavy shrubbery we didn't notice this before."

"We didn't investigate this side of the house," Shannon said. "We walked by it but the undergrowth was too thick to see anything."

"You weren't looking for a door," Travis said. "I doubt Louise knew about this. She never mentioned it."

Max looked around. "Someone knew about it. How?"

"Probably someone who's lived here his whole life and knows these houses," Travis said.

Shannon frowned. "We surely would have heard someone hacking the bushes."

Charli shook her head. "Not if they did it the day Travis and I went to Rouen, when you were in London."

Travis narrowed his eyes. "Or someone could have done it after Jeanne and Louise's deaths before you got here." His features tightened. "Baptiste was here alone for days fixing the plumbing. He had time to search, especially if he knew what to look for."

Charli grimaced. "Why didn't the person break into the room before now?" Like the sun peeking through scudding clouds she saw things clearly. "He, or someone, did break in, although they couldn't get into the house with the tower door locked. I thought some of the trunks looked like they'd been gone through, but I figured either Louise or Jeanne did it sometime before they died. The intruder wouldn't have found anything of value, other than the clothes. He, or she, wouldn't have been able to get into the safe, if they even knew it was there." She frowned at Max. "Did your vault guy mention it to someone?"

Max scratched his head. "That's not like Pierre. Others may have been watching and knew we'd called him in."

Shannon shivered. "What do we do now? The crook might come back."

"We'll board up the door, as I suspect it was before the culprit discovered it," Travis said. "If our trespasser comes back, he can't get in this way again."

Excitement churned through Charli, giving her new energy. "While you work on the door, Shannon and I will go through the letters we found in the safe."

They might finally solve a few mysteries.

# CHAPTER FORTY-ONE

The sound of hammering as Travis and Max boarded up the hidden door provided background noise to Shannon and Charli, seated at the kitchen peninsula, sorting through the letters from the safe.

Charli held up a packet of letters. "I've got the ones in Louise's handwriting." Travis had pointed them out to Charli.

Shannon looked up. "Two different handwritings on these. They look masculine. I wish we could read French."

"Me, too. Travis can translate them easily, but he's busy and we need to start now."

Charli snagged her phone off the counter. "I'm going to try to translate some of these."

"Okay. I'll make us tea." Shannon headed to the stove. She grabbed the teapot and filled it with water, then turned on the gas burner.

"Oh, my God."

"What?" Shannon whirled around and stared at her.

"I scanned this first letter and let the app translate. It's to Édouard. Louise tells him she's pregnant and wants money from him or she'll tell Adele."

"Blackmail! That's a classic reason to commit murder."

Charli translated another letter. Widening her eyes, she held up the letter. "This is addressed to Baptiste. Louise asks for the same amount of money in her letter to Cantrell, but she tells Baptiste she'll go to the police and tell them what he did if he doesn't pay her." Charli dug through the letters and pulled out another one. "This is addressed to the village police, and it's in Louise's handwriting."

"Maybe she's letting the police know what Baptiste did." The teapot whistled and Shannon turned off the gas. She leaned against the counter. "More blackmail and another motive for murder. The plot thickens. Wonder why Louise made copies of those letters."

"Probably insurance in case something happened to her. She must not have trusted either man." Charli rifled through the pile again and pulled out a yellowed envelope. "This one looks old. It says 'confession' on the front. That word is the same in French and English."

"This is huge," Shannon said. "What does the 'confession' letter say?"

Insides churning, Charli translated. "Wow! This is from Maurice stating he cut the breaks on Dominique and Andre's car, causing it to crash. He's confessing to their murder."

She scrubbed a hand down her face, trying to digest all she'd read. "Let's think about this. Édouard is married, but his wife knew about Louise. Getting his mistress pregnant might make Adele ask for a divorce, and maybe Édouard wouldn't want that because he needs Adele's money. I can't see him as a killer though. Baptiste doesn't seem like a killer either, but Louise held something over him, maybe an old crime."

Shannon moved from the stove. "We need to tell Travis and Max."

A popping sound came from outside. The women stared at each other.

Dread and fear surged through Charli. She jumped up from her seat. "I've never heard gunshots but that's what it sounded like."

The front door slammed and Charli released a breath. "Must have been a car backfiring. Here are the guys now." She looked toward the door with a smile for Travis and Max.

Instead, Baptiste, holding a gun aimed at her, stood there. Charli's vocal chords froze and her heart plummeted to the vicinity of her knees. She clutched the edge of the peninsula to steady herself. Her fingers pressed into the cool granite.

Shannon screamed and dropped the mug she held. It crashed to the floor, shooting fragments of ceramic everywhere.

Charli found her voice. "What do you want?" From the corner of her eye, she spotted movement from Shannon.

"You! Stop and get over there." Baptiste brandished the gun at Shannon.

Shannon sidled next to Charli.

"You! It's you who's the culprit? What the hell?" Charli fought to stay calm. "Where are Travis and Max?"

He chuckled, the sound evil in the quiet room. "They aren't going anywhere for a long time."

"What did you do to them?" Sweat beaded on Charli's forehead. Her pulse sped up.

"Never mind them." He glanced at the papers strewn on the counter. "Give me those. I want the necklace too. I watched this place and saw the vault specialist. I know you opened the safe. Louise told me the ruby necklace was in there."

Charli lifted her chin. "Why do you want them?"

He laughed again. "Not very smart, are you? The necklace will bring me a lot of money. Those letters are evidence I killed Louise."

"You? Why?" Charli suspected the reason, but she had to keep him talking.

"She threatened to tell the authorities of a past deed. I did not want to go to prison."

"What past deed?" Charli asked.

"I can tell you because you won't be alive to alert the police. Once, in a moment of weakness after Louise and I made love, I confessed to a murder I committed in Paris. The man was wealthy, and I'd swindled him out of a lot of cash. He was going to turn me in, so I killed him. I used the money to move back here and set up my business."

"Louise told Cantrell she was pregnant and the baby was his. She was blackmailing him, same as she was blackmailing you."

"Bah! Cantrell is an idiot. I watched him knock Louise unconscious and steal the diamond necklace. It was nothing for me to strangle her."

His malevolent grin made the fine hairs on Charli's arms stand at attention. "You and Cantrell both killed her?"

He shrugged. "Cantrell made it easier for me. Louise came to and tried to fight when I was strangling her, but she was no match for me. Now, be good girls and hand over the letters and the necklace."

"How do you expect to get away with this?" Shannon asked. "You just confessed to murder, several murders."

"You'll die in the fire I set to this house. I knocked out Gardner and shot his man. When Gardner wakes up, it will be too late." His hate-filled voice echoed through the room.

Travis was alive. Thank God. She and Shannon needed to make a run for it. Charli folded her arms across her chest. "Why should we give you anything if you're going to kill us anyway?"

He moved closer, his stance menacing. "Give me what I want and your death is swift from my bullet. Give me nothing and you burn slowly. It's up to you."

"You were the one who broke into the turret room last night." *Keep him talking, Charli.*

Baptiste waved the gun. "You thought you were clever to

change the locks. But I'm smarter. I found the escape door when I was here to fix your plumbing. No more talking. Give me what I want."

The women began scooping up the letters and stuffing them into the plastic box they'd found earlier. "The necklace isn't here," Charli said. "It's in my room."

"Then we will all go to your room." Baptiste held out a hand for the box.

Their only hope was to make an escape out the front door on their way to her room. Charli handed him the box.

Baptiste gestured with his gun for them to lead the way.

Suddenly, the teapot filled with boiling water flew across the room and hit Baptiste in the shoulder. He screamed, brushing at the hot water splattered across his arm and chest, when a body shot into the kitchen and tackled him, knocking him to the ground and sending his weapon and the box of letters flying.

Travis.

Charli yelped and jumped out of the way of flailing arms and legs. She glanced to the ceiling where Andre and Dominique floated, even more transparent than before.

"Andre threw the teapot," Dominique said. "We could not let that monster kill you."

Charli's heart beat triple time. She thought it might burst out of her chest. The two men struggled together on the floor. Travis had Baptiste by the throat but Baptiste fought him off and both staggered to their feet.

The men pummeled each other. Charli heard the crack of bones. Blood dripped from Baptiste's nose and she guessed it had broken.

Charli suddenly remembered the gun. "Where is it?" She spotted it on the floor by the sink. She dove for it. She'd never held a gun before. Gripping the weapon with both hands to stop her trembling, she aimed it at the men. "I have a gun and I *will* shoot!"

She couldn't get off a shot and risk hitting Travis. Shannon snatched a vase off the counter. Nodding at Charli, she circled the fighting men. Charli held the gun, ready to fire.

Baptiste knocked Travis to the floor and fell on top of him. Shannon crashed the vase over Baptiste's head, then jumped back. He shook his head and straightened, releasing his hold on Travis. He stumbled toward Shannon.

Charli fired the gun.

Clutching his arm, Baptiste dropped to his knees. Travis grabbed Baptiste and pinned him to the ground. Max, blood seeping through his shirt from a shoulder wound, held his gun and lurched into the kitchen. A cut on Max's forehead trailed blood down his face.

Max studied the scene before him. His thin lips formed a slight smile. "Looks like you've got everything under control." He fainted.

# CHAPTER FORTY-TWO

Charli flopped onto the sofa in the study. Travis handed her a glass of wine. She sipped the silky smoothness, then set the glass on the low table. The chaos was thankfully over. The police had come and arrested Baptiste for Louise's murder, the assault on Travis and Max, the attempted murder of Shannon and Charli, and breaking and entering.

Travis translated the letter addressed to the police. In it, Louise said Baptiste had confessed to the murder in Paris. Charli gave the letter to the police. No doubt Baptiste would also be charged with that killing.

Paramedics treated Travis for the head wound he'd received when Baptiste attacked him. He promised them he'd go to the hospital for a scan of his head later that day. They stabilized Max and took him to the hospital, saying he should make a complete recovery. Max had been at the back of the house getting more boards when Baptiste snuck up on Travis and knocked him unconscious. Baptiste waited for Max to come around to the front, where he shot him. Before Max could fight back, Baptiste knocked him out with one of the wooden boards Max had dropped.

Travis was torn between wanting to go to the hospital with Max or stay with Charli, but Max insisted he stay to help Charli.

Travis sat next to Charli and wrapped his arms around her, drawing her close.

"I'm glad that's over, but I can go without that kind of excitement for the rest of my life," she said. "I'm not sure I want to watch any more of my crime shows now that I've been in the middle of the real thing."

He laughed. "We're all okay, and that's what's important. Although Max's ego took a hit that he allowed Baptiste to attack him."

She faced Travis. "Baptiste was sure you'd be out for hours. Thank God you came to when you did."

He frowned. "I felt a blast of cold air on my face. It woke me up."

Charli glanced across the room to where the ghosts sat together on one of the upholstered chairs. They nodded, and she smiled her thanks. Then they disappeared. The ghostly specters were dimmer. Their unselfishness in sacrificing much of their essence for her and Travis melted Charli's heart. She hoped they didn't have to spend eternity in Purgatory.

Snuggling closer to Travis, Charli said, "I'm glad the police picked up Édouard for being an accessory to Louise's murder, and for theft." She laughed. "He started singing like a canary, as they say in the movies. Thank God Édouard gave the police the pearl and diamond necklace. The police assured me they'd return it to me as soon as they were able. The necklace Adele and Édouard said they'd had made to look like Jeanne's really was hers. They're holding Adele for receiving stolen goods. I should have realized it was the same necklace."

"You're a trusting person so took their word the necklace Adele wore was a copy. I'm sorry for Jeanne," Travis said. "She was a good person. If not for Édouard, we wouldn't know the truth. If Jeanne hadn't argued with Louise about Louise's out-of-control spending perhaps she wouldn't have had the heart attack. Jeanne might have survived if the paramedics were called right away, but Louise left her lying there for almost an hour. In a sense, Louise killed Jeanne. All very sad and sordid."

"The deaths gave me this place and brought you into my life, but at a high cost."

Édouard had told the authorities that after Louise and Jeanne argued, and Jeanne collapsed, Louise took the jewelry. She was wearing it when she and Édouard fought in the garden. When she fell unconscious, he stole the necklace.

Travis kissed Charli's forehead. "What will you do now?"

"Have everything assessed and put the house on the market."

"You'll go back to Philadelphia?"

She wondered if she imagined the regret in his voice. "That's always been the plan."

"Plans can change, Charli."

<><><>

In the three weeks since Baptiste and Édouard had been arrested, Charli quit her job and sold the couture clothes they found in the turret to a Paris collector who promised to have a showing. She'd had the clothes assessed and was pleased with the money she received. The promise of a showing made Dominique happy. Monsieur Belanger, at Charli's direction, contacted Sotheby's to auction the tapestry, the wine, and other items of value she didn't want. The expert who assessed the tapestry declared it could go for upwards of thirty thousand dollars. She decided to give the new clothes and accessories that had belonged to Louise to a charity for abused women.

The story of the arrests and of the long-ago murder of Dominique and Andre made headlines all over France. Charli accepted interviews, mainly to expose the truth behind the spirits' deaths. A French filmmaker indicated his interest in doing their story.

With Travis's help, Charli packed the Frank Stella painting and the portrait of Dominique and Andre and shipped them to Chloe's gallery in Philadelphia.

Surrounded by packing boxes in the living room, she stood up from the floor and grabbed her bottle of water off a table. She'd decided to keep small, personal items, framed photos, autographed books decades old, some of the Art Deco jewelry, all reminders of her family's heritage. She decided to take the necklaces, too, and sell them when she got home.

Sadness threatened to overwhelm Charli, and she sank onto the sofa. In the past weeks, Travis had spent every day at the manor helping her and Shannon with the inventory.

He'd spent every night in Charli's bed. Their lovemaking had taken on a bittersweet desperation in the knowledge this might be the end of their time together. She wanted him in her life, but she worried she confused love with her new sexual awakening. Her long-held fear of loving someone too much also held her back. Everything that had happened in the weeks she'd known him was unreal, not part of her world. Until she was sure of her feelings, she'd continue with her original plans.

The front door opened and closed. She recognized Travis's footsteps headed toward the living room. Charli ran to greet him.

He gathered her into his arms and held her tightly, then took her lips in a kiss that was as poignant as it was intense.

She pulled away and looked into his eyes. "Something is wrong. I feel it."

"Come, let's sit." He took her hand and led her to the sofa, pulling her down to sit next to him.

"What is it?" she asked.

"I have good and bad news."

She caressed his face. "Tell me all of it."

He drew an audible breath. "I've been offered an important job in Germany. Now that Louise's murder is solved, I can concentrate on my career again."

"Travis, that's wonderful. What's the bad news?"

"They want me right away. I leave tomorrow morning, and I'll be gone several months." He cupped her face between his hands. "Hear me out. I know you leave for Philadelphia within the week. Tonight will be our last time together. For a while."

He released her and got down on one knee on the floor. He held her hand. "Charlotte Deveraux, I love you with all my heart. I will always love you. I want a life with you. Please marry me."

Tears streamed down her face. "Travis, I love you, too, but I'm afraid. So much has happened. I need time to sort out my feelings. Deveraux Manor and Normandy are like a dream. I worry I've been swept up in this new world that's not real. Things may seem different when I'm back in my real world. I don't want to lose you, but I don't want to hurt you. You're a good man, and you deserve the best in life."

Still holding her hand, he sat next to her again. With his free hand, he swiped away her tears. "This is your world, Charli, in Normandy, with me. I restore art. You restored me."

"Give me time. Please."

"I'll give you time, but I'm an impatient man."

Charli wrapped her arms around his neck and kissed him with all the love that filled her heart, the love she feared.

<><><>

The ghosts, cloaked from Charli, flitted back and forth across the ceiling.

"Mon Dieu," Dominique cried out. "All our work. Gone. For nothing. Is Charli crazy? She belongs with Travis. We have failed again. We will spend eternity in that place, and Charli and Travis will never know the true love that burns between them."

Andre grabbed his wife to him and held her close. "Settle down. All is not lost."

## CHAPTER FORTY-THREE

"Charli, don't forget that meeting with Sadie Laplante's agent today." Chloe Decker DiMarco stood in the storeroom doorway where Charli was busy inventorying supplies for their gallery in Philadelphia's Society Hill.

Charli wiped her hands down her jeans. "I remember. I need to go back to my apartment and change. To sign her for a showing will be quite a coup."

"It sure would, and I have you to thank for going after her."

"What are partners for?" Back in Philadelphia two months, Charli had sold the necklaces at Sotheby's and made enough to buy into Chloe's gallery. The manor and grounds still hadn't sold, but once they did, she'd have a nice nest egg to build on. Her dream had come true, but it felt empty. She missed Travis more every day. She didn't believe it possible to have her heart torn to pieces.

Chloe studied her with transparent gray eyes. "Heard from Travis lately?"

Charli leaned against a shelf. "I haven't heard from him in a week, which is unlike him. He's called me almost every day since

I left France, and now silence. Maybe he's fallen out of love with me."

"If you love him, you need to go to him. Don't let him get away. I should know."

"I'm happy you and Matteo found each other again."

"We went through some heartache, but we made our relationship work. You and Travis can, too."

"I realize now I love Travis deeply, but my feelings for him scared me. I've kept busy selling the necklaces, finding a new apartment, and buying into the gallery, and I let time get away from me. I don't want to give up this gallery, but I need to be with Travis, too. How do you and Matteo do it, living in two countries?"

Chloe smiled. "We love each other."

After Chloe left, Charli stood frozen, her thoughts tumbling over each other, for long minutes. It hadn't seemed that simple for her and Travis, yet she couldn't take the lonely nights or days without him. She'd been a fool not to accept his marriage proposal. But she'd wanted to be sure. Now that she knew her heart, she hoped it wasn't too late.

She pulled out her phone to do what she'd been contemplating for a long time. Monsieur Belanger picked up on the third ring. "Monsieur, this is Charlotte Deveraux."

"Bon nuit, Charlotte. Good news. We had a very generous offer on the manor today. I was just about to call you."

"I appreciate all your help, and I hesitate to tell you this, but I've decided to hold off on the sale."

"*Quoi?*"

Even if she didn't recognize the French word for "what," the shock in Belanger's voice would have clued her in as to what he said.

"I'll pay your commission, and a little extra, but I'm not sure I want to sell. I'm coming back to Normandy. I'm coming home."

Calmness settled over Charli. She was going home, to Normandy, where she belonged. To Travis.

Smiling, Charli said goodbye to Belanger and hung up.

"It's about time."

At the French-accented female voice, Charli sprang back several feet. Hand over her heart, she whirled to face Dominique and Andre, with Angel held in Andre's arms.

"You gave me a fright," Charli said.

Andre chuckled. "It is nothing like the scare we gave all prospective buyers at Deveraux Manor."

"You haunted the house? Is that why we've had no offers despite a very competitive price?"

"But, of course," Dominique said. "We knew you would eventually realize you need Travis and Deveraux Manor."

Charli's heart rate slowed. "What are you doing here? I thought you never left France. Apparently, you didn't frighten everyone away. Monsieur Belanger has a substantial offer on the house. Good thing I called him when I did." She dropped onto one of the desk chairs.

"We can leave France any time," Dominique said. "We choose not to because to travel far takes a good deal of our essence, but you need us."

"You're almost completely transparent now," Charli said. "That's not good, is it? What will happen to you? You've helped us so much I don't want you to lose yourselves."

"Do not worry about us," Andre said. "Whatever we sacrificed is worth it to see you and Travis happy."

"We have found it is a beautiful thing to make others happy." Dominique crossed herself. "That is the message God wanted us to learn."

"I wish I could hug you both," Charli said.

"As do we," Dominique said.

Andre smiled. "Now that there is a serious buyer, some *nouveau riche* Americans who didn't respond to our haunts, we had to hurry to Philadelphia before the sale could be finalized. You recognized on your own that you love Travis and the manor."

"I do." Charli looked from one to the other. "Have you seen him?"

"He is well, but he misses you." Dominique gave her husband a slow smile and touched his arm. "We will leave now. We have never been to Philadelphia and we are anxious to explore. There are many old buildings that need haunting. We can scare people without exposing ourselves. We'll have fun one last time before we go back to the holding place." She rolled her eyes. "Your Mr. Ben Franklin constantly extols the virtues of his city."

With that, the ghosts disappeared.

Chloe came into the room and glanced around. "I thought I heard voices."

"I was on a call to the attorney in France." Charli held up her phone. "I've taken the house off the market for now. I'm going to Travis, if he'll still have me. I'm getting ready to book the first flight to Paris." She chewed her lip. "That meeting today. I can't leave you in the lurch."

Chloe grabbed Charli in a hug. "Don't be silly. I can handle the meeting on my own. Go to Travis, my friend."

# CHAPTER FORTY-FOUR

"*A*bout time you came to your senses." Shannon stood in Charli's bedroom later that day, watching her pack for her trip to France on an overnight flight.

Charli turned to her. "I had too much going on, and I had to be sure. I didn't want my heart broken again, and I didn't want to hurt Travis." She grimaced. "He hasn't called in a week. Has he given up on me?"

"That man loves you."

Charli's apartment security phone rang. She started for the kitchen to answer, but Shannon shooed her away.

"I'll get it."

"Thanks. Probably my doorman telling me I have a package."

On her way to her dresser to pull out some sweaters, Charli skimmed fingers over the portrait of Dominique and Andre that hung in her room. "You two are the best." The Frank Stella graced her living room wall. Despite offers to sell it, she couldn't part with it.

She went back to her packing. Shannon came into the room.

"What was it?" Charli glanced at Shannon.

"He called the wrong apartment." Shannon's face reddened, and she stooped to pick her purse off the floor. "I need to go."

"I thought we were ordering a pizza before you drive me to the airport."

"Be back in plenty of time. Just remembered something I meant to do."

Charli shrugged and turned to her suitcase. She heard the apartment door open and close.

"Hello, Charli."

At the crisp British voice, Charli gasped, dropped the sweater she held, and spun around.

Travis stood in the doorway, looking sexier than a man had a right to. Like a woman starved, her eyes devoured him, taking in his black leather jacket, untucked white shirt, faded jeans, and boots.

Unable to move, she licked her dry lips.

Travis started toward her. Her body came alive, and she flung herself into his arms, holding onto him with all her strength.

Laughing, he hugged her close, then pulled away to cup her face between his hands. "I've missed you more than I thought it possible to miss anyone."

She linked her arms around his neck and stared into the eyes of the man she loved. "I've missed you, too. When I stopped hearing from you, I thought you didn't love me anymore."

"I could never stop loving you. I wrapped up my job in Germany a few days ago and prepared to come here." He smiled. "I was afraid if I talked to you by phone, I'd let it out I was coming, and you'd tell me not to, that you'd moved on and found someone else. I had to see you, to beg my case, if needed."

She placed a tender kiss on his lips. "I love you so much. I'll never want another man. The answer I should have given you months ago is yes."

Travis put his finger on her lips. "No regrets. I want to do this again." He got down on one knee and held her hand. "Charlotte Deveraux, will you marry me?"

"Yes, yes."

He stood and grabbed her around the waist, swinging her until she laughed so hard tears streamed down her face.

"Come with me." He took her hand and led her into the living room.

His suitcase rested on the floor by the door. Travis dug into the case and pulled out a jewel box. He opened it and held it out to her.

A ring rested on the white satin. The pear-shaped diamond, large and brilliant, sparkled in the overhead light.

Travis took out the ring and placed it reverently on Charli's finger.

She turned her hand, admiring the way the light caught the gem, bouncing tiny prisms of rainbows on the white walls.

"Do you recognize the diamond?" he asked.

"It looks familiar." She widened her eyes. "Is it? Could it be…?"

He gently took her shoulders and pulled her closer. "It's the diamond from Jeanne's necklace. I'm having the pearl chain made into a necklace for you. I thought you might want to leave the ruby one as is."

Charli's heart thumped hard. "You bought them from Sothebys? That's why they sold so quickly, and for more than we asked."

"I didn't want you to lose your heritage."

Joy exploded in her. She grabbed his upper arms. "You are the best man in the world. I have news. I'm not selling the manor yet until I know what I want to do. I can't let it go. Or let France go. And I especially can't let you go. Home is wherever you are."

His eyes softened, and he bent to take her lips in a kiss, hot, intense, filled with love. After several passion-filled minutes, they pulled apart. Their breathing harsh, they clung to each other.

He gently pushed her away and held her at arms' length. "Let's get married soon, Charli. I don't want to wait."

"I don't either."

"There are two guests I want to invite to the wedding."

"Sure. Who?"

"My father and brother. Loving you has enabled me to put aside my differences with my dad and open my heart to him. I have you to thank."

"Travis, I'm so happy, for you, for us."

"We're good for each other. It will always be that way."

"Kiss me."

He took her into his arms for a kiss that promised a lifetime of passion, love, and dreams fulfilled.

# CHAPTER FORTY-FIVE

"My heart is full, mon amour." One month later, Dominique and Andre sat on a table in the elegant French restaurant in Philadelphia where a small but joyful group celebrated Charli and Travis's wedding. Because their essences had gotten low, they dared not appear to Charli.

"We did good, ma cherie. We completed our mission. Charli and Travis have embraced their destiny, Louise's murder is solved, and the world now knows Maurice killed us." Andre pointed upward. "Maybe we can go to the good place now."

Dominque placed her hand over his. "Most of all, we learned to put others before ourselves, what He wanted all along. Do you think we can get back the essence we lost, and do you think He will let us stay here and help others find their destiny? I love making others happy and bringing people together."

"We will ask His angel. I think maybe the answer will be yes." Andre kissed her tenderly. "After all, we are the best matchmaking spirits who ever lived. Or died."

<><><>

Married at a small historic church in Philadelphia's Old City, Travis and Charli joined their best friends and a few art patrons of the gallery, for dinner in a private room at the trendy and stylish restaurant. The newlyweds toasted each other with rich French champagne.

"Happy, Mrs. Gardner?" he asked.

"Delirious, Mr. Gardner."

"Looks like everyone is enjoying themselves, even Max." Travis nodded across the room to where Max was deep in conversation with one of Philadelphia's wealthiest society mavens, a patron of the gallery. Sitting at the table with Max and the woman was Travis's father Hubert and brother Tate. The two Gardner men had made the rounds of the guests, talking to each person, smiling, happy.

"I think your dad and Tate are having a good time," Charli said. "I'm glad they came."

"I am, too. They love you almost as much as I do."

Charli's gaze swept the room. At one table, Chloe leaned her head on her husband's shoulder, while Shannon laughed at something Niall Fraser said. He'd come from London to see Shannon and attended the wedding.

Shannon glanced away, and Charli followed her gaze to Travis's brother. Shannon and Tate had been trading looks all evening. Interesting, Charli thought.

"Looks like Shannon and Niall are getting cozy," Charli said to Travis. "Tate seems interested in Shannon, too."

Travis kissed her lightly on the lips. "Enough about the others. We've got an exciting life ahead of us."

"One I'm fully ready to embrace. I'm no longer afraid to take chances, thanks to you."

"You ready to handle the gallery alone when Chloe and Matteo head to Italy next month?"

"Of course, but I won't be alone. You'll be here, and we have good help at the gallery."

He gathered her against him. "The job in New York won't take long, and it's close enough to commute to Philadelphia. I've lined up several jobs in Europe for when you can go with me, including the painting restoration at the DiMarco villa."

Charli would run the gallery the times Chloe and Matteo were in Italy. When Chloe returned to the gallery, Charli would accompany Travis to his jobs. He felt she'd be a help to him, and she was looking forward to it. They'd decided Travis would sell Beliveau, and they'd make Deveraux Manor their home.

She snuggled closer to her new husband. They might have to make adjustments as they went, but their love would carry them through the bad times, and the good.

She pulled his head close. "I love you."

They kissed to claps and cheers from their friends. Travis released her, and Charli sighed with contentment. Her life had come full circle, and she wouldn't have it any other way.

Ghostly specters shimmered from across the room. For a flash, she could see Dominique and Andre. Charli lifted her champagne flute in a silent toast to the generous spirits who'd sacrificed so much to help Travis and her. The ghosts of Deveraux Manor.

### THE END

READ Chloe and Matteo's story in *Curating Love*, coming 2020

SEQUEL TO CHLOE and Matteo's story, *Ravello Marriage Bargain*, coming 2020

# ABOUT THE AUTHOR

*An award-winning and eclectic author, Cara Marsi is published in romantic suspense, paranormal romance, and contemporary romance. She loves a good love story, and believes everyone deserves a second chance at love. Sexy, sweet, thrilling, or magical, Cara's stories are first and foremost about the love. Treat yourself today, with a taste of romance.*

*When not traveling or dreaming of traveling, Cara and her husband live on the East Coast of the United States in a house ruled by two spoiled cats who compete for attention.*

Visit Cara's website at www.caramarsi.com to read about her books and to sign up for her newsletter.

Follow her on Facebook, Instagram, and BookBub:
www.facebook.com/authorcaramarsi.com
www.bookbub.com/authors/cara-marsi
https://www.instagram.com/carolyn2829/

Storm of Desire

Sweet Temptations

Sweet Temptations Boxed Set

The One Who Got Away

The Ring

Wedded in Vegas (Gambling on Love Book 1)

Love by Chance (Gambling on Love Book 2)

A Very Vegas Christmas (Gambling on Love Book 3)

The Gambling on Love Trilogy

Wedding Dreams Boxed Set

MULTI-AUTHOR BOXED SETS

Brandywine Brides: A Blackwood Legacy Anthology

Sizzling Summer Boxed Set

The Marriage Coin Boxed Set

Read excerpts at www.caramarsi.com

All books available at online booksellers

A Catered Romance, A Groom for Christmas, Brandywine Brides: A Blackwood Legacy Anthology, Capri Nights, Cursed Mates, Franco's Fortune, Ghosts of Deveraux Manor, Logan's Redemption, Loving Or Nothing, Luke's Temptation, Murder, Mi Amore, Snow Globe Magic, The Gambling on Love Trilogy, The Marriage Coin, and Wedded On a Dare, are available in print

www.ingramcontent.com/pod-product-compliance
Lightning Source LLC
Chambersburg PA
CBHW020402210626
46816CB00006BB/2080